The Sixth Annual report of the Receipts and Expenditures of the City of Concord

Anatiposi

Anonymous

The Sixth Annual report of the Receipts and Expenditures of the City of Concord

Reprint of the original.

1st Edition 2023 | ISBN: 978-3-38230-548-2

Anatiposi Verlag is an imprint of Outlook Verlagsgesellschaft mbH.

Verlag (Publisher): Outlook Verlag GmbH, Zeilweg 44, 60439 Frankfurt, Deutschland
Vertretungsberechtigt (Authorized to represent): E. Roepke, Zeilweg 44, 60439 Frankfurt, Deutschland
Druck (Print): Books on Demand GmbH, In de Tarpen 42, 22848 Norderstedt, Deutschland

THE

SIXTH ANNUAL REPORT

OF THE

RECEIPTS AND EXPENDITURES

OF THE

CITY OF CONCORD,

FOR THE FISCAL YEAR ENDING FEBRUARY 1,

1859.

TOGETHER WITH OTHER ANNUAL REPORTS AND PAPERS
RELATING TO THE AFFAIRS OF THE CITY.

CONCORD, N. H.
INDEPENDENT DEMOCRAT OFFICE—FOGG & HADLEY.
1859.

THE

SIXTH ANNUAL REPORT

OF THE

RECEIPTS AND EXPENDITURES

OF THE

CITY OF CONCORD,

FOR THE FISCAL YEAR ENDING FEBRUARY 1,

1859.

TOGETHER WITH OTHER ANNUAL REPORTS AND PAPERS
RELATING TO THE AFFAIRS OF THE CITY.

CONCORD, N. H.
INDEPENDENT DEMOCRAT OFFICE—FOGG & HADLEY.
1859.

REPORT OF THE COMMITTEE ON FINANCE.

The Joint Standing Committee on Finance, in conformity with the requirements of the ordinance prescribing their duties, " establishing a system of accountability in the expenditures of the city," submit to the City Council their Annual Report of the receipts and expenditures of the financial year, ending February 1, 1859 :

We have examined the Treasurer's books, and those of the City Clerk, and find that all payments therein recorded, are authenticated with proper vouchers, and the several items, footings, and balances correctly cast.

RECEIPTS.

The revenue of the year has been derived from the following sources :

By balance in Treasury, Feb. 1, 1858,							$1049·34
am'nt received of J. L. Cilley, taxes,					1854,		43·68
"	"	" B. F. Gale,	"			1855,	164·81
"	"	"	"	"	"	1856,	360·00
"	"	"	"	"	"	1857,	7,700·00
"	"	"	"	"	"	1858,	33,770·72
By stone sold off farm,							226·30
rent of city hall,							28·50
account of pauper,							4·00
Chichester, for paupers,							12·14
amount returned from pauper,							6·50
rec'd of State Treasurer, balance of R. R. tax,							550·29

By Charlotte Woolson, premium on bond, — 90·00
Matthew Harvey, " " — 45·00
Josiah Cooper, interest on legacy of A. Walker, — 60·00
Caleb Page, premium on bond, — 23·00
John Abbott, license, — 3·00
Ellinor Fiske, premium on bond, — 46·83
P. H. Seavey, " " " — 24·42
Richard Bradley, " " " — 99·16
Enoch Gerrish, " " " — 25·00
L. D. Stevens, Admr. on estate J. Whipple, — 177·29
Moody Kent, premium on bond, — 104·67
Shepherd & Sloat, license, — 50·00
J. H. Wilkins, premium on bond, — 54·67
Chandler Eastman, premium on bond, — 54·67
dividend on Mechanics' Bank shares, — 16·00
Literary Fund for 1858, — 674·36
Enoch Gerrish, premium on bond, — 28·08
Mary G. Stickney, " " " — 112·33
Ellen A. Seavey, " " " — 29·75
Charles Minot, " " " — 62·50
Joseph Moody, liquor agent, — 10·00
J. Abbott, sale of old iron, Concord bridge, — 5·50
J. C. Tebbets, premium on bond, — 69·17
County of Merrimack, for paupers, — 999·86
Charlotte Woolson, premium on bond, — 37·17
Railroad tax, 1858, — 3628·61
John Abbott, dividend on bank shares, — 16·00

$50,463·34

EXPENDITURES.

The expenditures of the year have been as follows, chargeable to the respective appropriations, viz:

Paid State tax,	$2408·00
county tax,	5370·72
school tax,	8275·36
school-house taxes,	4977·00
teachers' institute,	137·40
city paupers,	1046·81
county paupers,	725·76
roads and bridges,	3822·65
interest and principal of city debt,	5350·00
superintendent of highways,	6000·00
police and watch,	970·39
incidentals,	1149·78
fire department,	1877·49
printing and stationery,	520·01
professional services,	120·00
streets and common sewers,	279·79
salaries,	3486·77
abatement of taxes,	229·26
parsonage fund,	279·16
outstanding parsonage fund of 1857,	106·20
cemeteries,	20·00
precinct,	449·21
repairs at city farm,	141·41
ward house in ward 2,	575·00
engine house in ward 3,	80·00

$48,398·17

The details of the expenditures, (with the balance of old accounts and the appropriations,) will be found under the several heads. Following which will be found a statement of the city debt, debts due the city, an estimate of value of property belonging to the city, including city farm and personal property, gravel lots, and the bridges; also reports of the Superintendent of Streets, the Chief Engineer of the Fire Department, etc., etc.

JOHN ABBOTT,
M. T. WILLARD,   } FINANCE COMMITTEE.
N. B. WALKER,

February 1, 1859.

EXPENDITURES

OF THE

CITY OF CONCORD,

FOR THE YEAR ENDING FEBRUARY 1, 1859.

STATE TAX.

Paid State Treasurer's warrant, $2408·00

County Tax.

Paid County Treasurer, $5370·72

For Schools.

Paid A. G. Dow, for district No. 1,			$136·24
Theodore F. Elliott,	"	" 2,	82·22
Moses H. Farnum,	"	" 3,	313·21
Franklin B. Carter,	"	" 4,	84·31
Reuben K. Abbott,	"	" 5,	95·70
Ezra Ballard,	"	" 6,	98·50
Joseph Hazeltine,	"	" 7,	114·60
Charles Hall,	"	" 8,	129·59
P. Brown, Union, (9, 10, & 11)			5585·96
George Turner, district No. 12,			221·61
William Hayward,	"	" 13,	125·52
Charles Graham,	"	" 14,	84·86
David P. Bachelder,	"	" 15,	81·32
A. Thompson,	"	" 16,	57·60
Thomas C. Capen,	"	" 18,	126·07
Marstin M. Tallant,	"	" 19,	180·41
Wm. H. Allen,	"	" 20,	473·95
John L. Tallant,	"	" 21,	106·07

Paid Jonathan L. Leavitt," " 22, 96·95
 Robert Hall, " " 23, 19·10
 Daniel D. Clark, " " 24, 51·55
 J. W. Page, No. 8, in Hopkinton, 3·48
 W. Odlin, district No. 18, in Hop-
 kinton, 6·54
           $8275·36

School-House Taxes.

Paid T. F. Elliott, dist. No. 2, for 1857, $156·00
 D. P. Bachelder, dist. 15, 1858, 25·00
 M. B. Abbott, dist. 18, for 1858, 346·00
 S. Seavey, Union District, 4200·00
 P. Brown, " " 250·00
           $4977·00

Teachers' Institute.

Paid George W. Gardner, $137·40

County Paupers.

Paid E. G. Kilburn, goods to paupers, $51·05
 E. C. Ferrin, wood " " 2 25
 T. J. Carpenter, aid to Peno family, 13 27
 John Abbott, fare of paupers, 23 85
 E. G. Kilburn, goods to paupers, 62 95
 H. H. & J. S. Brown, aid " 40 08
 J. M. Jones, wood to paupers, 11 50
 Wm. H. Smart, medical aid " 89 75
 John Abbott, paid for car fare, 8 00
 James M. Jones, wood, 16 47
 J. Abbott, car fare, of Mrs.
 Laragee, 15 00
 J. C. Trask, care of T. O. Smith, 40 00
 J. M. Jones, wood to paupers, 2 25
 E. G. Kilburn, aid " 62 58
 J. A. West, " " 29 00
 Hiram Simpson, car fare, 4 00
 Whittredge & Doty, goods to pau-
 pers, 3 00
 Bridget Larkin, care of T. Kieley, 3 00
 W. Odlin, goods to paupers, 8 27

Paid B. A. Vogler, taking care of child,   5 00
 Philip Peltier, " " Lucie Se-
  clair,   8 00
 Peter Nurey, " " Lucy Fre-
  mond,   8 00
 T. Haynes, Adm'r of J. J. Farring-
  ton,   47 50
 G. K. Knowles, funeral attendance, 2 50
 T. Haynes, medical services, 3 00
 C. A. Lockerby, med. att. on T. O.
  Smith,   63 00
 B. S. Warren, " " 17 50
 David Davis, rent of house, 30 00
 Wm. H. Smart, med. attendance, 14 00
 David Watson, cash paid transient
  person,   .   1 00
 Henry M. Moore, rent of house, 4 00
 Z. Arlin, support of Mrs. E. Ballard, 5 25
 Northern Railroad, fare of tran-
  sient persons,   17 85
 John Abbott,   "   " 7 55
 J. A. Harris & Co., shoes, 5 34

Carried to City pauper account, $725·76

City Paupers.

Balance of old account, $771 78
By appropriation April 3, 1858,   500 00
By County of Merrimack,   999 86

              $2271 64

Paid E. G. Kilburn, goods to paupers, $50 04
 Wm. H. Rixford, serving pauper
  notices,   12 00
 J. F. Sargent, medical service, 8 25
 H. Rolfe & Sons, aid to paupers, 25 00
 W. A. Swain, aid to J. D. C. Wheel-
  er,   13 00
 Plymouth, aid to Simeon Eastman, 16 94
 Joseph Brown, funeral expenses of
  Jas. Sargent,   11 00

Paid E. G. Kilburn, goods to paupers, $31 50

H. H. & J. S. Brown, goods to paupers,   27 88

T. J. Carpenter, goods to Mrs. Bar-
ton,   3 02

Manchester, support of Geo. W.
Berry,   17 53

Hiram Simpson, for oxen, $150 00,

"   "   paid Mrs. Taylor,   35 00

J. M. Jones, wood to paupers,   9 25

W. H. Smart, medical attendance,   39 50

Jeremiah Fowler, aid to paupers,   36 70

Wilson Dimick, aid to pauper,   15 00

J. K. Smith, aid J. D. C· Wheeler,   7 00

J. M. Jones, for wood,   4 62

Hall Roberts, rent of Mrs. Whitney,   2 00

B. F. Gale, aid furnished paupers,   58 23

Joseph Brown, funeral services of 3
paupers,   23 50

Asaph B. Hemphill, taking care of
A. Colby,   14 00

John Carter, board of sister to
June 6, 1858,   19 50

J. M. Jones, wood to paupers,   7 12

E. G. Kilburn, aid to paupers,   120 84

J. A. West,   "   "   12 56

Wm. Ford, board of Mrs. J. Smith,   18 85

Plymouth, aid to Simeon Eastman,   31 40

Henry L. Ferrin, wood to Mrs.
Goodrich,   4 50

Bullock & Willis, aid to paupers,   10 45

A. B. Hemphill, care of A. Colby,   11 00

John Putney, goods to Moses Sargent,   4 00

John A. Coburn, funeral expense of
Carter Elliot,   7 00

George F. Whittredge, goods to paupers,   10 68

Durrill Smart, milk to David R.
Tandy,   3 15

Town of Andover, medical aid to
Charles Arlin,   34 50

Paid John Abbott, car fare to Andover, $2 35
    John Batchelder, goods to paupers,   1 49
    Joseph Brown, funeral attendance
      on paupers,   13 50
    Asaph B. Hemphill, care of A. Col-
      by,   5 75
    D. Smart, milk to David R. Tandy,   3 30
    Timo. Haynes, Adm'r of J. J. Far-
      rington,   19 74
    G. K. Knowles, funeral of Mrs.
      Sanborn,   2 50
    Durrill Smart, milk to Tandy and
      Abbott,   6 00
    Town of Plainfield, support of Moses
      Morse,   37 67
    Rent of house for Tandy,   4 00
    Joseph Brown, funeral attendance,   22 00
    G. K. Knowles,   "   "   2 50
    John Carter, board of sister,   19 50

                      $1046 81
      County paupers,   725 76

                      $1772 57
      Carried to new account,   499 07

                                    $2271 64

Roads and Bridges.

By balance of old account, $1956 37
By appropriation April 3, 1858,   3000 00

                                  $4956 37

Paid Simeon Farnum, work on road, $16·79
    H. M. Robinson, 3 wheelbarrows,   7·50
    J. F. Day, breaking out road,   4·00
    Henry E. Dow, work on road,   17.37
    Sherman D. Colby, "   "   63·50
    A. B. Holt, for gravel,   67·75
    George Frye, work on road,   24·88
    Charles K. Fisk, "   "   23·98
    Matthew N. Brown, "   "   16·50

Paid H. Rolfe & Sons, timber and work
 on bridge, $83·00
Emerson & Cutting, plank,   3·66
H. H. & J. S. Brown, materials for
 bridge,   18·00
Simeon Farnum, breaking out road,   1·25
B. E. Goodwin, 381 feet of plank,   5·00
Blake & Emery, for turf and loam,   20·00
G. W. Brown, 2592 feet of timber,   31·10
Enoch Jackman, work on road,   14·72
John G. Kimball, "   "   3·12
Richard Bradley, "   "   5·00
John S. Durgin, snowing bridge,   6·12
Josiah S. Locke, breaking out roads, 11·38
Josiah Dow,   "   "   "   5·00
John Abbott, making new road,   360·61
C. L. Currier, breaking out side
 walks,   2·55
B. G. Davis, work on road,   4·00
Simeon Farnum "   "   6·00
J. T. Moulton, breaking out road,   3·00
S. M. Chesley, blacksmith work,   44·53
I. Silver, 7 1-2 days shoveling snow,   7·50
Henry M. Moore, land damage,   4·00
Henry L. Elliot, breaking out roads,   3·70
Amos Sawyer, snowing bridge and
 work on road,   14·50
Samuel B. Locke, land damage,   1·00
Wm. B. Hurd, work on road,   2·00
Hiram Simpson, "   "   4·95
A. C. Abbott, snowing bridge, &c.,   10·03
Geo. A. Pillsbury, edge stones,   18.37
Henry E. Dow, breaking road,   8·00
Geo. W. Flanders, work on road,   2·81
William Abbott, work on road,   5·25
A. Thompson,   "   "   10·65
James F. Ward, setting monument,   5·00
J. S. Abbott, work on road,   11·50
N. P. Rines, breaking out roads,   9·12
Thos. Potter, 1 day on Loudon line,   1·50
John Y. Mugridge, costs on pet. of
G. F. Whittredge, for new road,   93·00

Paid C. K. Fisk, breaking road, $6·40
 Henry Farnum, breaking out road,   3·60
 Geo. D. Abbott, 2 guide boards,   2·50
 George Frye, 3016 feet plank,   45·24
 A. W. Parker, work on bridges,   56·31
 Henry Martin, Jr., work on road,   14·10
 Eben F. Elliot, 7320 feet plank,   96·96
 Thomas T. Moore, land damage,   20·00
 W. H. Proctor, work on road,   27·75
 Reuben Goodwin, land damage,   190·00
 James Powell, building culvert,   40·00
 John Wheeler, drain in Centre st.,   175·25
 D. Tandy, drain in Cedar street,   248·55
 C. L. Brown, work on road,   25·00
 John Ewer, land damages,   120·00
 Eben F. Elliot, 5118 feet plank,   67·01
 Joseph Moody, land damage,   90·00
 David Davis, land damage in Myrtle
  street,   125·00
 Timothy Carter, work on road,   19·00
 Betsey Dow, land damage,   15·00
 David A. Morrill, damage to wagon,   12·00
 John T. Gilman, land damage,   10·00
 Milton G. Boyes, " "   125·00
 Chandler Choate, " "   65·00
 J. G. Kimball, work on road,   15·20
 A. G. Dow, " "   13·04
 George Foss, " "   27·25
 Geo. D. Abbott, 5 guide boards,   5·50
 Hiram and Daniel Farnum, making
  road,   667·43
 J. N. Flanders, work on road,   10·00
 George Foss, building road,   202·07
 John Richardson, plank for bridge,   5·11
 Thomas Eastman, land damage,   50·00
 Amos Hoit, work on road,   5·22
 Benjamin A. Hall, " "   2·00
 Gilman Colby, land damage and
  building road,   75·00
 George W. Frost, land damage,   37·00
 George W. Frost, 12 bound stones,   6·00
 E. Jackman, work on road,   7·30

Gust Walker, spikes, &c.,	2·37
Samuel Clifford, work on road,	3·80
Joseph Moody, timber,	3·50
M. M. Tallant, land damage,	12·00

	$3,822·65	
Carried to new account,	1,123·72	
		$4,946·37

Police and Watch.

By balance of old account,		$388·67
By appropriation April 3, 1858,		1,300·00
		$1,688·67

Paid John C. Hall, police service,	$6·00
Isaac Eastman, " "	6·00
George B. Elliot, " "	7·00
Wm. T. Locke, night watch,	69·50
E. E. Sturtevant, police service,	18·20
C. H. Norton, rent of Marshal's office,	75·00
S. C. Pickard, police service,	13·51
W. H. Buntin, " "	6·00
W. Stevenson, " "	9·00
Isaac G. Howe, " "	25·46
John A. Coburn, " "	8·52
B. F. Gale, " "	65·84
Hiram Simpson, police service,	3·00
W. T. Locke, night watch,	48·99
E. E. Sturtevant, " "	207·48
J. L. Pickering, ground rent of lobby,	25·00
F. Labonta, watchman,	84·52
James Hoit, use of land for lobby,	5·00
E. E. Sturtevant, watch,	208·62
W. T. Locke, watch,	77·75

	$970·39	
Carried to new account,	718·28	
		$1688·67

Printing and Stationery.

By balance of old account,		$157·59
By appropriation April 3, 1858,		500·00
		$657·59

Paid Morrill & Silsby, printing and stationery,	$36·58	
Fogg & Hadley, printing and advertising,	54·00	
Butterfield & Merriam, advertising,	29.25	
Fogg & Hadley, printing annual report,	130·00	
Fogg & Hadley, printing School Report,	65·00	
Rufus Merrill, binding,	12·98	
Geo. G. Fogg, advertising,	35·50	
G. P. Lyon, stationery,	9·87	
McFarland & Jenks, advertising,	76·36	
Jones & Cogswell, printing,	9·00	
J. A. Merriam, Agent, stationery,	21·72	
Fogg & Hadley, printing and advertising,	39·75	
	$520·01	
Carried to new account,	137·58	
		$657·59

Superintendent of Repairs of Highways and Bridges.

By balance of old account,		$200·00
By appropriation April 3, 1858,		6000·00
		$6200·00

Paid orders at different times,	$6000·00	
Carried to new account,	200·00	
		$6200 00

Incidentals.

By balance of old account,		$76·38
By appropriation April 3, 1858,		1500·00
		$1576·38

Paid A. J. Hook, work in hall, $19·58
 Gas Company for gas,   42·40
 H. Simpson, making water trough,   5·00
 O. F. R. Waite, engrossing amend-
  ment,   3·00
 W. T. Putnam, for gas fixtures,   6·57
 Seth Eastman, edge stones front of
  church,   65·50
 G. D. Abbott, setting glass,   1·75
 County of Merrimack, execution v.
  Concord,   2·57
 Peter Dudley & Son, horse hire,   5·00
 E. E. Sturtevant, lighting lamps,   6·00
 F. Coffin, carriage hire,   2·00
 John Abbott, post office stamps, &c.,   2·16
 Leonard Drown, work on lobby,   2·92
 Isaac G. Howe, repairing hearse,   29·00
 W. E. Chandler, cash for expenses,   26·00
 William Pecker, wood,   3·37
 Jacob Carter, P. O. bill,   1·06
 A. J. Hook, cleaning lobby and hall,   2·00
 John Abbott, cash paid witness,   10·41
 P. Carroll, sawing wood,   1.25
 John H. George, execution Day v.
  Concord,   83·51
 Nathan Wiser, for 14 trees and labor, 17·00
 B. F. Gale, various services,   13·82
 J. H. Quimby, work on fence round
  City Hall,   4·50
 Cyrus W. Paige, making fence,   56·14
 Merrimack County Mutual Fire In-
  surance Company, insurance,   —·84
 D. H. Fletcher, work on City Hall,   21·04
 E. Jackson, insurance,   62·50
 George Abbott, running line be-
  tween Dist. No. 2 and 20,   2·00
 J. B. Knox & Co., stamp for Mayor's
  office,   5·25
 David Watson, extra services,   18·74
 W. E. Chandler, for insurance,   31·25
 A. J. Hook, cleaning hall,   10·75
 Gas Company, lighting City Hall,   38·40

Paid Moore, Cilley & Co., wedges, drills,

&c.,	$4.56
Jonathan Eastman, surveying,	5·00
John Abbott, paid 3 small bills,	3·87
J. L. Lewis, repairing lightning rods,	2·00
Jacob Carter, P. O. bill,	57
M. T. Willard, 4th July celebration,	150·00
Nath'l White, water to City Hall,	7·50
Morse & Granger, lamp post at City Hall,	31·88
John T. Weeks, firing cannon,	6·00
S. Seavey, bulletin board,	1·00
Jacob Carter, post office bill,	1·50
Bullock & Willis, powder, &c., for cable celebration,	12·00
S. Moody, shingling hearse house,	5·19
Charles Smart, witness fees in Neally v. City,	14·45
John F. Nealy, agreement in suit,	50·00
E. Jackson, cash paid Dist. No. 10,	14·76
County of Merrimack, board of prisoners,	16·00
G. F. Whittredge, rent of hall 1 year,	20·00
David Hoag, mending slates on roof,	17·20
David Watson, making alphabetical list of marriages,	25·00
John Abbott, paid various bills,	16·39
Jeremiah S. Abbott, six cords wood,	30·36
A. J. Hook, care of City Hall,	2·50
Concord Gas Light Company,	30·80
Geo. Sanders & Co., sundries,	18·56
Edson C. Eastman, books to poor scholars,	2·88
B. L. Johnston, sundries,	5·03
City Library, per resolution,	50·00
Jacob Carter, post office bill,	1·50
	$1149·78
Carried to new account,	426·60
	$1576·38

Salaries.

By balance of old account, $1251·45
By appropriation April 3, 1858,   3500·00

                                      $4751·45

Paid Charles L. Batchelder, clerk Ward 1,	$5·00
Peter Sanborn, assistant police justice,	25·00
Timothy Haynes, health officer,	10·00
B. S. Warren, " "	10·00
George Frye, assessor, 7 days,	14·00
David Pillsbury, judge police court,	100·00
A. P. Tenney, superintending school committee for 1857,	17·00
John Batchelder, alderman,	35·30
Timothy C. Rolfe, common council,	22·10
J. F. Runnels, " "	25·50
William Pecker, " "	18·00
James Locke, " "	22·50
B. F. Holden, " "	19·50
Henry Farnum, " "	21·00
Richard Bradley, " "	16·50
C. W. Paige, " "	16·50
John Kimball, " "	14·30
N. B. Walker, " "	14·30
William Hart, " "	16·50
Stephen Webster, " "	16·50
Josiah Cooper, " "	18·00
Isaac Clement, " "	49·50
David Watson, city clerk, 1-2 years salary,	150·00
J. T. Hoit, clerk in Ward 2,	5·00
Austin Guernsey, clerk in Ward 4,	5·00
J. F. Chaffin, selectman in Ward 4, 2 years.	10·00
J. C. Abbott, " " 7,	5·00
J. C. Hall, " " 4,	5·00
W. H. Smart, city physician,	22·00
Benjamin Rolfe, selectman in Ward 6,	5·00
G. B. Elliot, selectman Ward 1, 3 years,	13·00
W. H. Allison, " " 6,	5·00
N. P. Webster, " " 7,	5·00
J. Locke, service on committee,	3·00
A. Hadley, clerk common council,	75·00
D. A. Brown, alderman 1857,	25·60
E. Dimond, " "	24·50
M. T. Willard, " "	17·60
E. Blake, " "	13·20

2

Paid W. Kent, alderman, 1857, 16·50
   G. F. Whittredge, " " 17·50
   J. Locke, selectman in Ward 2, 5·00
   W. E. Chandler, city solicitor, 100·00
   J. B. Curtis, selectman in Ward 2, 5·00
   R. Davis, alderman, 71·30
   J. N. Flanders, selectman Ward 3, 5·00
   Hiram Simpson, overseer poor farm, 350·00
   J. C. A. Hill, clerk in Ward 6, 5·00
   C. W. Batchelder, selectman Ward 5, 5·00
   H. G. Kayes, clerk in Ward 5, 5·00
   M. H. Johnson, selectman in Ward 7, 5·00
   N. W. Gove, clerk in Ward 7, 5·00
   W. Kent, service on committees, 40·60
   C. W. Paige, " " " 18·40
   W. Pecker, " " " 4·90
   W. Odlin, city treasurer, 100·00
   R. Bradley, services on committee, 17·62
   W. Hart, " " " 9·35
   H. Chase, selectman in Ward 1, 5·00
   T. Tenney, " " 2, 5·00
   A. Rolfe, superintending school committee, 15·00
   Charles Smith, superintending school com-
      mittee, 40·00
   G. F. Whittredge, services on committee, 30·90
   Joseph Hazeltine, superintending school
      committee, 25·00
   B. F. Gale, city marshal, 500·00
   I. Rowell, superintending school committee, 8·00
   G. W. Flanders, clerk Ward 3, 5·00
   Isaac Clement, services on committee, 20·80
   Henry Farnum, " " " 4·00
   T. C. Rolfe, " " " 5·10
   Josiah Cooper " " " 2·20
   John Abbott, superintendent of highways, 300·00
   B. F. Holden, services on committee, 9·10
   James D. Page, superintending school com-
      mittee, 6·00
   N. B. Walker, services on committee, 11·00
   M. T. Willard, " " " 18·40
   James Sanborn, selectman Ward 6, 5·00
   S. M. Vail, super'tending school committee, 43·00
   Albert Foster, assessor, 37·00
   J. F. Runnels, services on committee, 3·20
   Enos Blake, " " " 17·60
   Elbridge Dimond, " " " 16·40
   Leonard Drown, clerk in ward 1, 5·00

Paid J. S. McFarland, selectman in Ward 5, $5·00
   David Winkley, assessor,   36·00
   Sylvester Stevens, assessor,   16·00
   S. Seavey, making taxes,   28·00
   Hiram Simpson, in part,   125·00
   David Watson, 1-2 years salary,   150·00
   Amos Hadley, superintending school com-
     mittee,   30·00
   Henry E. Parker,   "   "   30·00
   Sewel Hoit, assessor in 1858,   32·00
   R. K. Buswell, selectman in Ward 3, 1857,   5·00
   George Frye, 11 days assessor, 1858,   22·00
   M. T. Willard, making taxes,   18·00
   J. Abbott, Mayor, 1858,   200·00

                                        $3484·77
     Carried to new account,   1266·68
                                                  $4751·45

Professional Services.

Balance of old account,   538·66
Appropriation,   300·00

                                        $838·66

Paid A. H. Bellows, term fees, Concord vs. Pills-
   bury, $40·00
   John Y. Mugridge,   3·00
   T. W. Gilmore, costs in Hubbard vs. City,   9·00
   M. W. Tappan, ser. in   "   "   24·00
   W. H. Bartlett, ser. Concord vs. Pillsbury,   12·00
   John A. Kilburn, ser. in State vs. Rogers,   24·00

                                        120·00
     Carried to new account,   718·66
                                                  $838·66

Repairs at Poor Farm.

By appropriation, April 3, $150·00
Paid Hiram Simpson, repairs, $109·77
   W. S. Reyburn, lightning rod,   31·64

                                        141·41
     Carried to new account,   8·59
                                                  $150·00

Fire Department.

By balance of old account, 1490·13
By appropriation, April 3, 1858, 1800·00

$3290·13

Paid engine company No. 2,	$217·50
Horace H. Holt, steward,	23·50
John A. West, articles furnished,	4·95
Engine company No. 3,	215·75
Luther P. Fuller, steward,	12·40
J. E. Hutchins, services,	8·12
J. S. & E. A. Abbot, repairs,	8·50
David A. Warde, keys,	4·17
Engine company No. 7,	116·75
Samuel Eastman, steward,	14·50
Engine company No. 8,	111·01
Hook and Ladder company,	162·50
Charles C. Shaw, repairs, etc.,	13·27
Gust Walker, lanterns, etc.,	17·38
D. W. Long, repair of hose,	36·59
A. B. Holt, fixing reservoir in Prince St.,	5·00
Wm. T. Locke, cleaning snow off reservoirs,	4·17
John D. Teel, steward of No. 4,	23·39
J. D. Johnson, badges for No. 4,	4·75
Lowell Eastman, lumber and services,	17·78
True Osgood, chief engineer's bill,	50·00
Five assistant engineers' bill,	25·00
Engine company No. 4,	218·00
Engine company No. 6,	91·60
S. M. Griffin, repairs on No. 2,	20·00
J. D. Wright, painting buckets,	2·00
Nathaniel White, water for No. 4,	2·50
Willard Williams, five leather caps,	5·62
A. T. Sanger, 8 glazed hats,	5·00
T. W. & J. H. Stewart, 8 rubber pants, etc,	34·84
George Dame, for firemen's collation,	187·50
A. H. Fellows, work on reservoirs,	29·45
A. H. Fellows and others,	5·25
T. B. Jones, 50 keys for No. 4,	9·00
E. R. Stevens, work on reservoir,	11·35
Concord, M. & L. R. R., freight of engine,	11·40
T. W. & J. H. Stewart, pants,	147·00

$1877·49
Carried to new account, 1412·64

$3290·13

Parsonage Fund.

Paid J. E. Lang, for North Cong. Society, $43·91
E. Jackson, for South Cong. Society,   31·43
Asa P. Tenney, for West Cong. Society,   19.11
G. W. Moulton, for East Cong. Society,   19·42
Gust Walker, for Unitarian Society,   30·84
N. White, for Universalist Society,   22·33
H. B. Foster, for First Baptist Society,   25·47
J. S. Crockett, for Pleasant st. Bap. Society,   11·64
H. C. Sanborn, for Methodist Society,   17·38
H. A. Brown, for Episcopal Society,   21·00
Josiah Cooper, for South Free Will
   Society,   8·20
T. C. Rolfe, Congregational Society at
   Fisherville,   9·15
D. A. Brown, for Baptist Society at Fish-
   erville,   12·50
J. B. Rand, for Methodist Society at Fish-
   erville,   6·77

                                       $279·16

Outstanding Parsonage Fund.

Paid North Congregational Society, J. E. Lang, $40·29
Unitarian Society, J. C. A. Hill,   29·41
Methodist Society, H. C. Sanborn,   15·76
West Congregational Society, H. Martin, Jr. 20·74

                                          $106·20

Streets and Common Sewers.

By balance of old account, $1616·60
Paid P. W. Watson, for edge stone, $7·50
James Hazeltine,   "   "   20·50
N. Call, damage to water pipes,   25·40
H. S. Shattuck, edge stone,   18·50
J. S. McFarland, "   "   8·25
M. C. Hadley,   "   "   3·84
W. H. Clark,   "   "   68·00
W. H. Clark,   "   "   127·80
                                —195·80

                                     $279·79
Carried to new account,   1336·81

                                       $1616·60

Abatement of Taxes.

Paid Caleb S. Rogers,	$4·20
Isaac Abbott,	9·20
Edward Ordway,	2·37
S. M. Chesley,	9·20
Lucy Maynard,	4·00
Durrill Smart,	5·28
W. W. Whittier,	2·08
Joseph Mansur,	5·89
Onslow Stearns, mistake,	110·04
George E. Sanborn,	7·00
John Page,	3·63
James Sanborn, bank stock,	5·85
Mitchel Gilmore, mistake,	3·50
Jehiel D. Knight, "	1·81
Hannah Whitney, "	1·71
Barney Mahan, "	3·51
Jacob Clough, "	2·10
Mary Abbott, over valuation,	4·68
H. A. Kendall, " "	8·75
C. A. Lockerby," "	4·60
C. H. Clough, " "	5·25
W. Gilman, mistake,	2·76
Lyman Sawyer, over valuation,	3·06
Joseph Spokesfield, mistake,	4·68
Esther Rand, over valuation,	4·10
Robert Eastman,	2·10
Isaac Eastman,	3·85
Harvey Chase, taxed in Hopkinton,	2·74
John F. Carter, mistake,	1·32
	$229·26

Principal and Interest of City Debt.

Paid principal,	$1000·00	
Interest,	4350·00	
		$5350·00

Ward House in Ward 3.

By appropriation,	$500·00	
" " additional,	75·00	
		$575·00

Engine House in Ward 3.

By appropriation,	$80·00
By timber left,	2·00
	$82·00

Paid C. & J. C. Gage,	39.50	
H. Rolfe & Sons,	2·50	
Warde & Humphrey,	6·31	
Chase, Ford & Co.,	10·37	
G. W. Brockway,	75	
Asaph Abbott,	13·00	
George Partridge,	4·00	
Samuel Holt,	5·39	
For trucking,	18	
		$82·00

Precinct.

Tax raised,		$550·00
Paid gas bill,	$131·84	
Morse and Granger, care of street lights,	50·17	
Morse and Granger,	28·75	
Gas bill to January 1, 1858,	198·45	
E. H. Ashcroft, gas burners,	9·00	
Wm. Gordon, care of street lights,	31.00	
		$449·21
Carried to new account,		100·79
		$550·00

Cemeteries.'

Paid R. W. Martin, painting hearse,	20·00

Indebtedness of the City, Jan. 1, 1858.

Funded debt,		55000·00
Note to N. H. Savings bank,	2000·00	
Union bank,	1000·00	
M. G. Stickney,	2000·00	
T. A. Harraden,	1500·00	
H. M. Robinson,	1000·00	
Nathaniel White,	1000·00	
Abigail B. Walker,	1200·00	
Eleanor Fisk,	800·00	

Bonds to the amount of $19,000·00 were authorized   19,000.00
by the City Council, May 1, 1858, for the purpose of   ———
funding the floating debt, and building Concord Bridge, $74.000·00
which were appropriated as follows, viz :

Amount brought over,	$74,000·00

Paid Eleanor Fisk, note and interest,		$849·45
N. H. Savings Bank, note and interest,		2083·67
Union Bank, " "		1038·33
Mary G. Stickney, " "		2074·50
T. A. Harraden, " "		1565·75
H. M. Robinson, " "		1072·33
Robert E. Pecker, " "		220·00
Nathaniel White, " "		1083·87
Abigail B. Walker, " "		211·40
Abigail B. Walker, " "		1048·67

Concord Bridge account :—

Paid proprietors for franchise,	1500·00	
E. L. Childs & Co., building		
bridge, as per contract,	4225·00	
roofing, extra,	169·00	
masonry 60·00, 367 ft. timber, 3·67 63·67		
removing old bridge,	22·63	
		5980·30

	17,228·27
Cash in Treasury,	271·73
	$17,500·00

Paid bond due January 1st. 1859,	$1000·00	
Bonds unsold, (of the $19000)	1500·00	
		$2500·00

Present indebtedness of city, Feb. 1, 1859,	$71,500 00

Assets of the City.

City Hall and half building,	$35,000·00	
City Farm, real and personal property,	10,721·18	
Gravel lot on Warren street,	350·00	
Gravel lot bought of Robinson & White,	2000·00	
Receiving tomb,	250·00	
Legacy of Abiel Walker, for schools,	1000·00	
Four shares of Mechanicks' Bank,	400.00	
Due from Pembroke, on acc. Concord bridge,	1000·00	
Balance due from B. F. Gale, taxes of 1857,	1894·87	
" " " " 1858,	12,182·24	
		$64,798.28

Inventory of Property at City Hall Buildings.

Gas fixtures for city part,	$393·95
76 settees,	279·13
6 stoves and 412 pounds Russia funnel,	140·00
Furniture in Mayor's and Common Council room ; chairs, desks, table, etc.,	305·25
2 wood boxes,	6·00
Stationery,	15·00
	$1139·33

Inventory of Property at City Clerk's Office.

1 long writing table, 6 drawers,	$10·00
2 large cases,	24·00
1 pine desk $2·00, one book case, $2·00,	4·00
1 small trunk, $1·25, 1 clock, $7·00,	8·25
2 lamps, can, torch, shovel, tongs, etc.,	3·50
1 copy Compiled Laws,	1·83
1 copy Geology of New Hampshire,	2·50
20 volumes N. H. Reports,	50·00
1 Bell's Digest,	2·50
	$106·58

Inventory of Property at City Marshal's Office.

27 police badges,	$33·75
1 writing desk,	12·00
1 stove and funnel,	10·00
1 long table,	6·00
1 clock,	5·00
8 lanterns,	4·50
2 set of handcuffs,	2·67
1 copy N. H. Compiled Statutes,	1·83
1 book case and table,	175
1 lock and six keys for Marshal's office,	1·75
2 locks and eight keys for lobby,	2·75
Shovel, tongs, axe, broom, snow shovel, pitcher, chairs, and other indispensables,	5·00
Stationery, etc.,	3·00
Bedding at lobby,	5·00
Curtains for Marshal's office,	3·00
	$98·00

Bridges.

	Built.	Cost.	Present Value.
Free Bridge,	1849–50	$16,753	$11,000
Federal Bridge,	1850–51	15,950	11,000
2 at Fisherville,	1849–50	5,150	3,500
Horse Hill Bridge,	1852	2,676	2,000
Sewall's Falls "	1852–53	8,070	7,500
Concord "	1858	6,000	6,000

——— $41,000·00

Engine-Houses with Apparatus, &c.*

Engine No. 2,	$1503·13
" " 3,	1867·75
" " 4,	2421·53
" " 6,	1125·18
" " 7,	1057·96
" " 8,	1630·01
Hook and Ladder Co.,	416·27

——— $10,121·83

$118,947·81

* The above valuation was made in 1854; but the additions since made, it is believed, will more than counterbalance the loss by wear and tear since that time—$450·00 having been appropriated for that purpose during the past year.

Taxes for 1858.

State, county, city, school and highway taxes,	35,381·23
Non-resident taxes,	400·95
School-house taxes,	9,301·98
Precinct tax,	$445·51

$45,529·67

SIXTH ANNUAL REPORT

OF THE

COMMITTEE ON THE CITY FARM.

To the Board of Mayor and Aldermen:

The undersigned, Joint Standing Committee on the City Farm, having attended to the duty assigned them, of taking an inventory of the property of the Farm, respectfully submit the following Sixth Annual Report:

Appraised value of farm and buildings in 1858,	$7630·00
" " " personal property in 1858,	3201·14
" " " improvements	49·00
Total,	$10880·14
Appraised value of farm and building in 1859,	$7630·00
" " " personal property, in 1859,	2941·18
Improvements in addition to house,	150·00
Total,	$10721·18

Number of paupers at the farm, Feb. 1, 1859,	21
Average number for the year,	21
Whole number for the year,	67
Died,	3
Sent to house of correction,	4

The receipts and expenditures for the past year will appear from the report of the overseer.

An addition to the house of a room for the sick has been made the past year.

The Committee find the farming operations well managed,

and neatness and order apparent in the household department, and the inmates as comfortable and happy as their varied habits and dispositions will admit.

Respectfully submitted,

ELBRIDGE DIMOND,
TIMOTHY C. ROLFE, } *Committee.*
ISAAC VIRGIN,

Inventory of Real and Personal Property belonging to City Farm, Feb. 1, 1859.

Farm and buildings,	$7630·00
Improvement,	150·00
	$7780·00

1 horse,	$110·00	1 horse rake,	8·00
4 oxen,	300·00	1 horse collar and chains, &c.,	3·00
6 cows,	210·00	50 casks and tubs,	15·00
1 2 year old heifer,	25·00	Beetles and wedges,	2.00
4 yearlings,	36·00	3 grind stones,	6·00
7 sheep,	25·00	1 hay cutter,	5·00
10 hogs,	65·00	Board logs,	10·00
18 tons English hay,	234·00	55 cords wood,	192·50
16 tons brook hay,	144·00	Oak timber,	20·00
2 tons corn fodder,	18·00	Lumber,	6·00
3 tons straw,	25·00	1 sleigh and harness,	25·00
64 lbs. butter,	10·00	2 wagons,	80·00
88 lbs. lard,	14·67	9 plows,	38·00
60 lbs. dried apples,	3·60	3 harrows,	15.00
90 doz. candles,	14·40	1 cultivator,	3·00
30 lbs. tea,	9·00	4 hay forks and 5 hay rakes,	3·25
4½ bbls beef,	67·50	1 hand rake,	50
3½ bbls. pork,	87·50	4 ox yokes,	11·00
152 lbs. ham,	19·00	4 augers,	1·50
85 lbs. fresh beef and pork,	8·50	1 saw sett,	80
1 bbl. vinegar,	6·00	2 chisels,	1·20
¼ bbl. pickles,	4·00	6 chains,	6·00
7¼ bbls. soap,	36·25	1 iron bar,	1·00
5 yards flannel,	2·50	10 baskets,	3·33
200 bush. corn,	200·00	Square shave and steel trap,	2·00
16 bush. beans,	32·00	1 cross cut saw,	3·00
70 bush. oats,	35·00	1 set dry measures,	1·00
300 bush. potatoes,	120·00	1 hand saw,	1·00
20 bush. turnips,	5·00	2 buffalo robes,	16·00
2 bush. beets and carrots,	1·00	40 fowls,	15·00
24 cabbages,	2·00	16 boxes,	2·00
200 lbs. cheese,	20·00	1 pick,	1·00
2 bbl. apples,	4·50	2 ox carts,	80·00
1½ bbls. cider,	4·50	10 lbs. tobacco,	2·50
3 saws and 8 axes,	11·00	10 bushels rye,	10·00
2 shovels,	1·33	3 " India wheat,	2·40
5 scythes and snaths,	5·00	80 " leached ashes,	7·20
6 hoes,	3·00	8 " dry ashes,	1·00
4 manure forks,	3·50	200 lbs. cart tire,	2·00
1 winnowing mill,	6·00	1 gun,	4·00
1 stone drag,	1·75	½ bush. peas,	1·00
2 bush scythes,	2·00	150 lbs. fish,	5·25
1 " hook,	1·00	2 lbs. yarn,	2·00
2 sleds and 1 barrow,	10·00	Household furniture,	371·25
			$2941·18

Receipts at City Farm.

By cash on hand,	$1·22	¼ bush. cucumbers,	33
1 cord of wood,	4·50	1 pig,	2·00
1 pig,	2·00	Pasturing,	24·00
4½ bush. beans,	6·75	Green hides,	17·99
38½ pounds candles,	4·82	20 bushels oats,	10·00
1 cord of wood,	4·50	M. Humphrey, for use of land,	4·00
5 bushels corn,	5·00	19 pair of feeting,	5·70
3 pigs,	8·25	4 pigs,	10·50
Cash of city treasurer,	150·00	Poultry,	5·22
2 pigs,	5·00	Work,	24·00
20 bushels potatoes,	10·00	Cabbages,	2·00
2 " beets,	1·00	Shingles,	75·00
2 " corn,	2·00	Beef,	22·92
2 " turnips,	50	5 cord wood,	16·00
6 " potatoes,	3·00	1 yoke of oxen,	100·00
17½ lbs. tallow,	1·75	Milk,	62·50
1 bush. potatoes,	50	Lumber,	47·44
3 pigs,	7·00	Eggs,	8·00
1 calf skin,	1·00	2 calves,	3·75
36 pounds veal,	2·16	1 pig,	3·00
4 pigs,	12·00	9 cords wood,	36·00
½ bush. potatoes,	50	Butter,	4.46
1 cow,	30·00	10 bushel oats,	5·00
1 calf,	4·20	Cash for stone,	50
3 lambs,	5·50	1 gallon soap,	12
32 bushels oats,	16·00		
			$705.33

Expenditures at City Farm.

1 barrel flour,	$7·00	Blacksmith's work,	25
12 cups and saucers,	50	12 pipes,	06
12 knives and forks,	1·84	1 bush. onions,	1·20
3 pounds of saleratus,	21	¼ gross matches,	12
15 " of sugar,	1·80	1 barrel flour,	7·50
2 gallons of molasses,	75	1 pair shoes,	1·17
33 pounds tobacco,	7·00	41½ yards shirting,	3·73
7 " coffee,	1·00	1 pound sulphur,	10
12 bushels rye,	12·00	2 combs,	22
1 quart oil,	30	Shoeing horse,	13
1 axe handle,	25	1 kit mackerel,	1·75
Blacksmith work,	34	100 pounds fish,	4 00
1 kit mackerel,	1.50	Setting boilers and fixtures,	8·34
1 bag salt,	22	1 manure fork,	1·34
1 pair mittens,	50	1¾ tons plaster,	9·33
½ pound beeswax,	21	1 stove door,	30
1 box pills,	20	2 qts alcohol and camphor gum,	55
Shaving soap,	08	Blacksmith work,	58
1 chamber,	40	1 pair shoes,	1·50
6 oz. linen thread,	48	2 yards denim,	40
Cotton thread,	10	1 pound cream tartar.	40
½ doz. plates,	29	1 broad axe,	82
40 gallons of molasses,	12·00	2 quilts,	70
1 bottle of peppermint,	34	1 turkey,	1·00
Starch,	12	1 pair shoes,	1·63
Fresh fish,	1·37	2 rolls salve,	30
18 pounds sugar,	2·00	35 bush. leached ashes,	3·15
2 " raisins, ½ cassia,	46	6 pounds tea,	3·00

Item	Amount	Item	Amount
42 yards sheeting,	3·78	4 bags salt,	1·00
12 " denims,	2·00	2 pounds coffee,	25
2 thousand laths,	4·00	Blacksmithing,	25
Grass seed,	6·00	1½ bushels rye,	1·50
1 barrel mackerel,	11·57	Crackers,	1·00
3½ bushels rye,	3·50	Padlocks,	62
2 pair shoes,	2·05	Shoeing horse,	96
1½ bushels barley,	1·13	Work on cellar wall,	1·50
Sawing lumber,	87	4 pounds rice,	25
1 quart gin,	40	1 bag salt,	1·30
23 pounds, sugar,	2·14	Clothes for Mrs. Harvey,	3·12
Blacksmithing,	41	4 scythes, 2 rifles,	3·70
1 tin pail and can,	45	Saleratus,	53
1 quart peas,	12	Carding and spinning wool,	3·49
23 pounds dried apple,	1·84	Blacksmithing,	35
1 bushel rye,	1·00	Bed cord,	34
Mending harness,	10	Cream tartar,	40
1¼ yards print,	12	1 pitcher,	25
1 chamber,	50	Strainer cloth,	50
1 pair shoes and mending,	1·40	Knitting needles,	08
1 barrel flour,	6·50	1 barrel flour,	6·00
Ink, pens and paper,	28	20 pounds sugar,	2·00
10 yards denims,	1·67	Grindstone,	3·16
5 pound nails,	25	3½ bushels rye,	3·50
1 cow,	24.50	1 bag salt,	22
20 gallons molasses,	6·40	14½ yards print,	1·54
Whip,	67	40¾ yards sheeting,	3·67
Paint,	75	Cleaning clock,	50
Tin ware,	65	Rice and cream tartar,	62
5 pound of coffee,	70	Sulphur,	10
Garden seed,	40	26 pounds sugar,	3·05
2 bed cord,	84	4 qts. blueberries,	40
1 bag salt,	22	8½ days haying,	11·34
6 pound sugar,	75	Repairing saw,	35
School books,	1·02	40 pounds nails,	1·60
10 pound nails,	40	100 " fish,	4·00
4 quarts peas,	40	Thread and tape,	23
Paid J. Hook,	1·25	Shoeing oxen,	75
9 pounds apple,	90	Rennet skin,	25
Mending plow and chain,	50	9 pounds sugar,	1·00
Clothes for H. Anthony,	5·25	Pepper and cream tartar,	54
1½ bushels rye,	1·53	Blacksmith,	47
2 files,	20	5 pounds coffee,	75
Twine,	14	1 bag salt,	1·30
Castile soap,	34	For work,	50
Tin pail,	62	Wicking,	46
5 pounds spikes,	62	For nursing,	3·50
1 " pepper,	16	2 pair shoes,	2·00
Indigo and copperas,	16	1 qt., gin,	50
100 pounds fish,	3·50	Sawing lumber,	9·50
1 cask lime,	1·10	Ginger and saleratus,	19
Coffee and sugar,	2·87	Saltpetre,	06
5 hats,	80	Crackers,	2·00
1 chamber,	28	1 barrel flour,	7·00
Whitewash brush,	1·37	1 pair shoes,	92
Writing books,	20	Blacksmithing,	2·58
1 bonnet,	1·50	2 pair shoes,	2·06
2 barrels flour.	12·25	Setting tire,	67
Medicine,	50	Broom,	30
Thread,	18	¼ pound cloves,	06
1 pair pants,	1·00	Coffee and sugar,	1·80
7 yards checked cloth,	1·00	50 pounds nails,	2·00
Quilts and comfortables,	7·00	Fly poison,	20
4 pounds rice,	25	1 pound tea,	50
1 pound slippery elm,	30	7 pound sugar,	84
Mending wagon,	25	5½ yards cotton cloth,	4·65
Nutmeg, cream tartar and saleratus,	79	8 pounds coffee,	1·12
Rennet skin,	25	Glass and putty,	29
Bed pan,	75	18 pounds sugar,	1·48
Gun lock,	1·50	Stove funnel,	3·57
6 yards cotton cloth,	38	1 barrel flour,	7·00
1 bush. India wheat,	80	1 yoke of oxen,	94·00
19 pounds sugar,	2·00	Cassimere,	11·75
Shoeing oxen,	1·81	Cream tartar and sugar,	2·76
1 pair shoes,	75	Shoeing oxen,	2·12

6 yds., shirting,	57	Sugar,	2·08
3 pounds saleratus,	21	2 gallons molasses,	75
Thread,	15	Making yoke,	75
Threshing,	9·00	1 barrel flour,	7·50
1 kit mackerel,	1·50	Shoeing horse,	1·00
Saw and filing,	1·00	Wash basin,	50
1 quart gin,	50	Buffalo robe,	8·00
1 shovel,	1·12	Stationery,	50
2 pair boots,	5·75	Hoop iron,	83
Vest trimmings,	1·29	Paid freight for Davis,	37
Shoeing oxen,	1·34	Boots,	2·50
100 pounds shorts,	1·10	4 gallons molasses,	1·50
Shoeing horse,	1·25	5 pound coffee,	70
41 pounds tea,	11·76	1 box mustard,	08
2 " tea,	1·00	Shoeing oxen,	3·08
Sewing,	7·00	Ledger,	1·75
1 barrel flour,	7·25	Stove and funnel,	1.25
Butchering,	2·00	7 bushels rye,	6·83
Sugar,	3·04	2 barrels cider,	5·30
1 quart oil,	25	Repairing axes,	2·75
4 bushels salt,	1·08	Sheeting,	95
2 barrels apples,	4·75	Blacksmithing,	85
1 coat,	5·00	Balance between cow and ox,	15·00
Mending plow,	1·33	1 barrel flour,	8·00
Sugar,	2·24	1 pound pepper,	16
8 rolls paper,	1·00	2 pound raisins,	30
Prints,	5·89	2 bunch shoestrings,	12
Blacksmithing,	34	10 pound sugar,	1·00
6 pounds coffee,	1·00	Newspaper,	1·50
Raisins and nutmeg,	67	Leech tub,	50
200 pounds fish,	6·00	Saleratus,	07
Pasturing,	24·00	Pant cloth and thread,	98
1 quart gin,	50	4 gallons molasses,	1·50
40½ yards flannel,	11·75	Blacksmithing,	29
32 bushel ashes,	2·88	Bottle peppermint,	33
2 doz. plates,	1·00	4 pounds coffee,	60
Hay cutter,	4·50	Cream tartar and saleratus,	42
Saleratus,	14·00		

$701·09

Amount of receipts at farm, $705·33
Amount of expenditures at farm,   701·09
Balance in the hands of Overseer, $4·24

REPORT

OF THE

SUPERINTENDENT

OF

REPAIRS OF HIGHWAYS AND BRIDGES.

The details of the expenditures will be found under the several heads of the appropriation appended.

JOHN ABBOTT, SUPERINTENDENT.

DISTRICT, No. 9, 27, AND 28.

Amount appropriated April, 1858, $1305·00

EXPENDITURES.

Paid for labor,

James Thompson,	$10·76
Calvin Worth,	90·25
Geo. McLear,	30·00
Owen Tweeman,	96·25
West Robinson,	124·00
Wm. Ahearn,	101·25
Geo. W. Garvin,	84·50
B. K. Abbott,	30·67
James Weeks,	132·43
S. L. Currier,	105·81
Wm. Robinson,	68·25
Patrick Larkin,	145·25
Cornelius Driscoll,	28·00
John Murphy,	110·75
Charles O'Brien,	62·45
Charles Butters,	161·32
John Cook,	25·00
Asa J. Hook,	58·86
Daniel S. Webster,	210·65
John Burke,	73·25

Paid for labor :

Charles Butters, nails, plank &c.,	20·70
Wm. T. Lock,	268·43
C. F Carswell,	317·30
Dexter W. Smith,	59·81
Michael Dolan,	20·50
Michael Gurley,	141·00
Samuel Simpson,	28·50
Foster Marsh,	38·25
Sullivan Mills,	82·50
Daniel Brown,	15·25
Jeremiah Brown,	132·50
Thos. Curley,	72·25
Harvey Hayes,	59·50
Patrick Morrison,	37·50
James Hicks,	41·50
N. P. Webster,	156·62
John Mills,	1·00
J. H. Haynes,	8·75
F. L. Tandy,	4·50
G. W. Ordway,	2·50

Paid for labor:

David Tandy,	4·50
Charles H. Tandy,	5·25
Nathan Wiser,	2·00
Thomas Morrison,	1·00
Thomas Murphy,	15·50
Thomas Upham,	5·00
Edson Miller,	3·50
Warren Abbott,	2·50
Joshua Palmer,	65
Geo. F. Whittredge,	94
Edward Carroll,	8·00
L. A. Walker,	24·25
Alexander & Sargent,	2·20
James Hook,	1·50
Patrick Glenning,	17·25
Waterman Dimond,	1·00
Richard Lee,	50
Smart & Sewell,	116·18
John Ballard,	2·50
Daniel Sanborn,	8·98
Gilman Judkins,	63·37
R. M. Ordway,	3·43
David White,	38·20
J. G. Hook,	15·08
J. W. Law,	1·50
J. L. Pickering,	6·50
W. J. Bachelder,	1·00
Frank Griffin,	1·00
J. M. Jones,	155·18
Wm. Prescott,	3·50
A. G. Saltmarsh,	12·00
Wm. Nichols,	4·50
John Wheeler,	26·00
Nath'l Abbott,	6·75
John Ewer,	10·00
Robert Knowlton,	1·40
Moses Sargent,	50
Daniel Law,	4·50
Isaac Abbott,	3·25
Joseph Keyser,	3·37
Cutting & Emerson,	2·09
Henry M. Moore,	3·50
Samuel Jenness,	3·15
Jacob Moulton,	1·63
Moses Brown,	30·25
Albert G. Dow,	7·60
Moses Carter,	4·00
Abbott Saltmarsh,	2·55
Robert Hall,	14·50
Warde & Humphrey, hardware,	55·82
Roby & Son,	1·65
Jacob T. Moulton,	1·00
Russell Hills,	3·85
John Potter,	50
Samuel Runnels,	3·82
B. K. Hall,	16·00
Moses Ordway,	2·00
Wm. Abbott,	4·50
Concord, Gas L. Co.,	7·81
Joseph Colby,	1·00
J. F. Runnels,	1·05
Cyrus Cass,	50·50
S. M. Chesley,	16·83
J. F. Hoyt,	2·00
W. T. Lock, sundries, bill,	44·00
Jefferson Pettengill,	3·75
Dexter W. Smith,	4·50
P. Cary,	2·75
J. Holt,	1·00
D. D. Clark,	3·50
Patrick Larkin,	8·00
Michael Gurley,	3·52

Abel B. Holt,   59·52

$4220·75

Balance not expended Feb. 1. 1851,   84·2₅

DISTRICT No. 1.

Amount appropriated April, 1858, $50·00

Paid for labor:

Reuben Goodwin, Surveyor,	$13·87
Jeremiah C. Elliot,	2·20
Joseph Cochran,	1·50
Aaron Q. Farnum,	3·30
Isaac C. Boyes,	1·63
Chandler Choate,	1·77
A. J. Smith,	38
Charles Smith,	38
Zebulon Smith,	4·40
Joseph F. Gage,	1·24
Thomas T. Moore,	3·30
Joseph H. Emery,	56
John H. Durgin,	38
Samuel Hutchins,	3·34
Josiah H. Hutchins,	65
J. P. Boyes,	3·57
Levi Lock,	38
James Lock,	3·39
Barnard Currier,	73
John T. Gilman,	2·00
John C. Danforth,	1·03

$5000·00

DISTRICT No. 2.

Amount appropriated April, 1858, $30·00

Paid for labor:

Enoch Jackman,	4·05
Caleb Gilman,	1·00
Joseph Moody,	5·75
Wm. Hayward,	2·90
John Ewer,	8·25
C. A. W. Folsom,	4·95
Z. W. Gleason,	1·00
Henry S. Gleason,	2·00

$30·00

DISTRICT No. 3.

Amount appropriated April, 1858, $47·00

Paid for labor:

Joseph Graham, Surveyor,	$13·62
Samuel C. Danforth,	1·00
Daniel Cutting,	1·00
Isaac Virgin,	5·50
Isaac F. Hoit,	80
Andrew Moody,	3·89
Charles C. Moody,	34
Lyman A. Hall,	1·50
Geo. G. Virgin,	4·35
David Sargent,	1·59
James C. Bartlett,	1·14
James C. Ewer,	2·97
Benj. Gale,	3·30
Charles Graham,	4·86
Geo. Graham,	34
Wm. Davis,	41
Charles G. Virgin,	34
Robert A. Brown,	55

$47·00

DISTRICT No. 4.

Amount appropriated April, 1858,	$44·00
Paid for labor:	
John G. Kimball, Surveyor,	4·19
S. S. Robinson,	6·19
Thompson Tenney,	2·97
David P. Batchelder,	68
Thomas D. Potter,	4·91
Samuel Kimball,	4·75
Charles V. Stockbridge,	1·91
Henry H. Potter,	6·27
Jacob A. Potter,	4·78
Nathaniel G. Wiggin,	5·48
Amos Sleeper,	1·25
David Bartlett,	62
	$44·00

DISTRICT No. 5.

Amount appropriated April, 1858,	$72·00
Paid for labor:	
David A. Morrill,	5·57
Amos Paul,	2·41
John L. Tallant,	17·00
Lemuel Smith,	3·00
Sylvester Stevens,	3·00
John B. Sanborn,	7·25
H. C. Adams,	4·44
James Hodge,	50
J. F. Hoyt,	3·25
Daniel E. Gale,	3·50
Abraham Bean,	8·00
	$61·98
Amount not expended Feb. 1, 1859,	10·02

DISTRICT No. 6.

Amount appropriated April, 1858,	$230·00
Paid for labor:	
Joseph Clough, Surveyor,	$16·00
Gardiner Tenney,	1·00
James Frye,	11·30
George Moody,	3·50
Benjamin Ambrose,	1·00
J. A. Merriam,	8·50
Washington Hill,	3·50
William Pecker,	7·50
Joshua Sanborn,	2·00
James Blake,	9·50
Heman Sanborn,	5·70
Mary L. Pecker,	3·00
Isaac Eastman,	16·00
Winthrop St. Clair,	2·50
William Page,	2·50
James Sanborn,	5·00
Jacob Clough,	2·00
John Jarvis,	2·20
Isaac Emery,	1·50
Samuel Eastman,	50
Smith Bean,	50
Wm. Page,	50
Peter C. Virgin,	1·50
George W. Moody,	3·00
David Parker,	1·00
James Blake,	2·50
E. S. Curtis,	2·71
Joseph Batchelder,	8·50
Pearson Clisby,	50
Samuel Curtis,	69
Benj. V. Adams,	1·00
James Sanborn,	1·00

J. A. Merriam,	2·00
John Eastman,	6·00
Samuel G. Potter,	2·00
Geo. W. Frost,	1·00
Harrison Bean,	1·00
Eli Hibbard,	1·00
John Sanders, Jr.,	1·50
Wm. Frost,	2·28
John B. Curtis,	5·15
John J. Eastman,	1·00
	$151·03
Amount not expended Feb. 1, 1859,	78·97

DISTRICT No. 7.

Amount appropriated April, 1858,	$20·00
Paid for labor:	
Josiah S. Locke, Surveyor,	4·91
Benjamin E. Badger,	·46
Samuel M. Locke,	35
Samuel B. Larkin,	4·64
Samuel B. Locke,	5·30
	$19·66
Balance not expended,	34

DISTRICT No. 8.

Amount appropriated April, 1858,	$29·00
Paid for labor:	
Abbott Saltmarsh,	5·87
John F. Carter,	31
John S. Coffin,	1·21
Asa R. Chamberlain,	38
John Davis,	55
Sylvester Davis,	31
Hiram Davis,	39
J. F. Day,	1·78
Alonzo Gates,	56
Jonathan Fellows,	72
Wm. C. Greenough,	51
Malachi Haynes,	33
Samuel C. Jenness,	31
Barter Holt,	62
Gilman Holt,	1·06
Augustus Holt,	31
Samuel C. Jenness,	75
Sam'l Jenness,	1·39
Cyrus S. Jenness,	34
Ira P. Kempton,	31
Jonathan P. Leavitt,	1·35
Thomas H. Morrill,	33
Jesse Morrill,	33
Benj. Morrill,	32
Samuel Haynes,	31
Jacob S. Moulton,	38
Nathan Pingrey,	68
George Sargent,	58
LaFayette Stevens,	68
Josiah Stevens,	1·56
Seth W. Saltmarsh,	37
George W. West,	46
B. S. Prescott,	97
William Abbott,	2·03
Newell Davis,	68
	$29·00

DISTRICT No. 10.

Amount appropriated April, 1858, $145·00

Paid for labor:

Hiram Farnum, Surveyor,	62·89
Michael Jenkins,	3·50
Moses H. Farnum,	5·00
Geo. W. Brown,	19·32
Wm. H. Brown,	6·62
Benj. Morse,	6·00
Charles H. Clough,	5·00
Benj. Brock,	1·50
Wm. H. Boutell,	1·80
Michael Kelley,	5·00
Asa P. Tenney,	2·00
B. F. & D. Holden,	1·00
Benj. Farnum,	14·37
Timothy Hoit,	4·50
John Lynch,	2·50
Franklin Varney,	4·00
	$145·00

DISTRICT No. 11.

Amount appropriated April, 1858,	$23·00

Paid for labor:

David Abbott, Surveyor,	$6·58
Gardiner Knowles,	41
Asa A. Blanchard,	7·48
Alfred C. Abbott,	4·72
B. F. Varney,	3·40
Jonathan Arlin,	41
	$23·00

DISTRICT No. 12.

Amount appropriated April, 1858,	$350·00

Paid for labor:

Francis Hoyt, Surveyor,	276·58
Seth B. Hoyt,	2·00
Jesse Morgan,	1·07
James Hoffman,	53
John Batchelder,	3·08
John Howard,	3·50
J. P. Saunders,	2·24
Charles H. Fitch,	38
Thomas Gahagan,	1·78
Andrew Keenan,	38
Allen & Hall,	2·26
Samuel G. Noyes,	1·92
John P. Hubbard,	3·51
Francis Runnels,	1·00
Charles Wallace,	38
H. Rolfe & Sons,	17·75
Benj. Morrill,	3·75
Moses H. Fifield,	2·78
	$325·89
Amount not expended Feb. 1, 1859,	24·11

DISTRICT No. 13.

Amount appropriated April, 1858,	$49·00

Paid for labor:

H. L. Elliott, Surveyor,	$7·00
Lewis B. Elliott,	80
Andrew Goodwin,	50
Jeremiah Fowler,	3·00
Luther M. Hoit,	50
Benj. Hoit,	4·00
Ezra Waldron,	85
James C. Elliott,	3·00
Eben O. Morrill,	39·00
Rufus D. Scales,	2·60
Chellis C. Elliot,	66

Peter F. Elliot,	91
Eben F. Elliott,	4·00
Luther B. Elliott,	1·23
Charles H. Currier,	40
Eli Elliott,	2·60
Aaron Elliot,	5·00
Joseph E. Scales,	4·50
Warren W. Whittier,	3·20
Theodore F. Elliot,	80
Ezekiel F. Elliott,	1·60
Geo. F. Sanborn,	1·46
	$49·00

DISTRICT No. 14.

Amount appropriated April, 1858,	$29·00

Paid for labor:

Geo. Foss, Surveyor,	7·24
Geo. Hoit,	34
Amos Hoit,	4·25
Ephraim C. Elliott,	1·70
Sylvester Hoit,	34
M. C. Elliott,	34
Thos. Eastman,	4·12
Josiah Hardy,	2·29
Alfred A. Eastman,	34
Hiram Eastman,	34
Sherman D. Colby,	2·00
Gilman Colby,	2·15
Solomon Colby,	34
Solon Sanborn,	3·21
	$29·00

DISTRICT No. 15.

Amount appropriated April, 1858,	$22·00

Paid for labor:

Harvey Chase, Surveyor,	$6·00
George B. Dimoud,	1·40
Samuel Runnels,	3·40
Luther Runnels,	36
Ephraim Swett,	1·00
Erl Colby,	1·35
Andrew P. Bennett,	46
Robert Knowlton,	5·00
Anna Runnels,	1·55
Andrew Crockett,	1·48
	$22·00

DISTRICT No. 16.

Amount appropriated April, 1858,	$38·00

Paid for labor:

Albert G. Dow, Surveyor,	$8·40
Robert B. Hoit,	9·48
John Sawyer, 2d,	83
Edward Runnels,	3·00
Josiah Runnels,	5·24
James H. Powell,	97
Joseph Runnels,	4·48
Edwin Terry,	1·08
Aaron Lamprey,	96
Amos Sawyer,	3·56
	$38·00

DISTRICT No. 17.

Amount appropriated April, 1858,	$29·00

Paid for labor:

R. R. Buswell, Surveyor,	$2·20

R. D. Ruswell,	50	Benj. Griffin,	1 00
John Fisk,	1·50	B. F. Griffin,	2·70
Jeremiah Abbott,	50	J. H. Ballard,	3·00
Wm. B. Thompson,	1·50	Ezra Ballard,	5·70
Wm. D. Colby,	2·50	Abira Fisk,	8·50
David C. Gile,	2·00	Charles Fisk,	2·00
Hazen Abbott,	3·50	E. B. Lane,	62
Moses M. Davis,	5·80		
John F. Elliott,	1·00		$40·00
Andrew Buswell,	1·50		
Samuel S. Buswell,	3·50		
Alvin C. Powell,	1·00	DISTRICT No. 22.	
Charles K. Fisk,	1·00	Amount appropriated April, 1858,	$49·00
Abiel Dow,	1·00	Paid for labor:	
		A. W. Parker, Surveyor,	$10·50
	$29·00	Benj. E. How,	2·00
		Charles C. Clark,	8.50
DISTRICT No. 18.		John Davis,	1·00
		Charles Hall,	16·00
Amount appropriated April, 1858,	$61·00	John Hall,	8·50
Paid for labor:		Samuel B. Hall,	50
John V. Aldrich,	$11·00		
Rufus Abbott,	1·05		$47.00
J. F. & H. L. Ferrin,	7·00	Balance not expended Feb. 1, 1859,	2·00
Nathan G. Spiller,	1·00		
Joseph Eastman,|	10·00		$49·00
Stephen Carleton,	4·00		
Hiram Simpson,	50	DISTRICT No. 23.	
Ira Rowell,	2·50		
J. & H. Farnum,	12·20	Amount appropriated April, 1858,	$73·00
Jacob Dow,	2·50	Paid for labor:	
Ezekiel Ferrin,	2·10	Wm. H. Proctor, Surveyor,	11·25
		Daniel Knowlton,	6·00
	$53·85	John Corlis,	1·56
Amount not expended,	7·15	S. L. Baker,	4·50
		I. P. Baker,	1·23
	$61·00	John Corlis, Jr.,	63
		R. West,	1·00
DISTRICT No. 19.		J. N. Abbott,	43
		F. P. Currier,	2·75
Amount appropriated April, 1858,	$30·00	Joseph S. Abbott,	16·48
Paid for labor:		Nath. D. Berry,	3·40
Henry Martin, Surveyor,	$11·19	Nathan Lovejoy,	1·90
Nathan K. Abbott,	5·06	Joshua Berry,	3·56
Jonathan Tenney,	1·50	Joseph Hazeltine,	1·93
Jehial D. Knight,	1·00	Wm. Bodwell,	1·10
Jeremiah S. Abbott,	5·50	Hiram Dow,	1·87
Reuben Abbott,	2·00	E. Dimond,	43
Reuben K. Abbott,	3·75	Wm. H. Currier,	43
		Stephen Currier,	1·37
	$30·00	H. B. Currier,	43
		John E. Proctor,	4·75
DISTRICT No. 20.			
			$73·00
Amount appropriated April, 1858,	$30·00		
Paid for labor:		DISTRICT No. 24.	
Jacob N. Flanders, Surveyor,	5·95		
Edward P. Farnum,	3·70	Amount appropriated April, 1858,	$22·00
George W. Flanders,	1·70	Paid for labor:	
S. R. Blanchard,	4·85	D. D. Clark,	$1·10
Daniel Dimond,	2·20	John Green,	86
Franklin J. Emerson,	5·00	Andrew S. Smith,	5·40
John E. Saltmarsh,	4·00	Benj. Green,	3·86
Levi Abbott,	2·00	Josiah Dow,	4·81
		C. Goodwin,	1·78
	$30·00	John Carleton,	1·90
		Alpheus Goodwin,	2·29
DISTRICT No. 21.			
			$22·00
Amount appropriated April, 1858,	$40·00		
Paid for labor,		DISTRICT No. 25.	
John Ballard, Surveyor,	$6·73		
David Farnum,	9·75	Amount appropriated April, 1858,	$78·00

Paid for labor:

Wm. Abbott, Surveyor,	$19·35
Charles II. Reed,	1·75
John C. Wheeler,	1·80
Benj. Wheeler,	2·60
Isaac F. Wheeler,	2·10
Ira Abbott,	3·70
Charles Abbott,	5·10
Daniel L. Saunders,	1·50
Thomas C. Capen,	4·85
Aaron Abbott,	2·10
Timothy Davis,	1·20
James Corliss,	55
Silas Messer,	4·80
Nelson Young,	1·05
David Hammond,	1·05
J. & M. B. Abbott,	23·60
Alfred M. Chandler,	1·00
	$78·00

DISTRICT No. 26.

Amount appropriated April, 1858,	$35·00

Paid for labor:

Geo. Frye, Surveyor,	$20·75
James How,	3·25
John Clark,	5·25
Thos. Tewksbury,	2·50
Sylvester Currier,	3·25
	$25·00

DISTRICT No. 29.

Amount appropriated April, 1858,	$27·00

Paid for labor:

Japheth G. Holmes,	$8·50
A. Thompson,	6·50
Jeremiah Mills,	1·19
David White,	3·30
	$19·49
Balance not expended Feb. 1, 1859,	7·51

DISTRICT No. 30.

Amount appropriated April, 1858,	$33·00

Paid for labor:

Timothy Carter, Surveyor,	$2·65
Augustine C. Carter,	6·50
Franklin B. Carter,	4·75
John Carter,	2·25
David Carter,	1·25
Elbridge Dimond,	5·75
Wm. Dimond,	1·00
Henry E. Dow,	2·60
Isaac H. Farnum,	1·50
Samuel Knowlton,	3·25
Geo. Abbott,	1·
	$33·00

DISTRICT No. 31.

Amount appropriated April, 1858,	$12·00

Paid for labor:

Reuben Meyers,	3·65
Joseph Lougee,	2·67
Samuel Clifford,	5·23
Geo. E. Lougee,	45
	$12·00

CHIEF ENGINEER'S REPORT.

To His Honor the Mayor, and the Board of Aldermen of the City of Concord :

In conformity with my duty as Chief Engineer, I would respectfully submit the following report:—

There have been during the past year, or since the first of last June, *fourteen fires and alarms*, as follows :

June 18.—Fire at Fisherville ; burning partially an out-building connected with the factory. Loss, $50·00. Covered by insurance.

Sept. 6.—Fire on the Concord Railroad, near the gas house, burning partially one car load of wood. Supposed to have been set on fire by one of the engines on the road.

Sept. 9.—False alarm given at the north end of Main street, by some person unknown.

Oct. 12.—Alarm caused by the partial burning of a lot of ties or sleepers on the Northern Railroad, above the Free Bridge road. Supposed incendiary.

Oct. 28.—Fire at the north end of Main street, burning a barn belonging to Mr. F. N. Fiske. Damage, $500. Insured for $200. Supposed incendiary.

Oct. 31.—Fire on the Fair Ground, at the south end of South street, burning a shed and partially burning a lot of boards stored in the shed, belonging to Mr. Nathaniel White. Damage about $200. Incendiary.

Nov. 2.—Fire on Monroe street, burning a house belonging to Mr. Loammi Gould. Damage, $500. Supposed incendiary.

Nov. 16.—Alarm caused by the partial burning of a pile of ties or sleepers on the Northern Railroad, near the Steam Mills of the Messrs. Holt. Supposed incendiary.

Dec. 10.—Fire burning the stable back of the Union Hotel, belonging to Mr. B. F. Dunklee. Damage, $650. No insurance. Accidental.

Dec. 11.—Fire in No. 2 engine house, extinguished without a general alarm by Mr. Roby and others who were in the house at the time. Cause, defect in the chimney.

Dec. 16.—Fire in the rear of the Elm House, burning the stable belonging to William M. Carter, and used by Mr. Foster, the proprietor of the Elm House, and Mr. John Neally. Damage about $200. Incendiary.

Dec. 17.—False alarm caused by the carelessness of the messenger sent to notify the foreman of No. 3 to come with 20 or 30 of the company to extinguish the burning hay which had assumed a dangerous appearance in the ruins of Mr. Carter's stable.

Dec. 27.—Fire between State and Main street, burning the shop and stable of Mr. John Chandler. Damage, $600. Supposed incendiary.

There was also a slight fire on the Concord Railroad, which was extinguished by Company No. 3, without giving a general alarm.

The fire apparatus of the city is located as follows :

CONCORD, No. 2.—Near the State prison, at the North end of State street ; has 550 feet of hose, in good repair. No. of members 60.

MERRIMACK, No. 3.—Near Abbott's Coach Factory, south end of Main street ; has 500 feet of hose in good repair. No. of members 60.

PENNACOOK, No. 4.—On Warren street ; has 500 feet of hose in good repair. No. of members, 60.

CATARACT, No. 6.—At West Concord; has 400 feet of good hose, and 100 feet of old hose. No. of members, 40.

OLD FORT, No. 7.—At East Concord, has 300 feet of hose in good repair. No. of members, 40.

PIONEEER, No. 8.—At Fisherville ; has 500 feet of hose in good order. No. of members, 50.

HOOK AND LADDER, No. 1.—Is located in the same building with Engine Company No. 4, on Warren street. No. of members, 50.

There are also two old engines belonging to the city ; one at the north, (No. 1,) the other, (No. 5,) at the south end, in the hands of young gentlemen from 15 to 18 years of age. These small engines, in many places in the city can, and no doubt will, do good service.

For the location of reservoirs I would refer to the Chief Engineer's report of 1857 and 1858. We have found it necessary during the past season, owing to the streets being raised, to raise the mouths of a number of the reservoirs, and cement them ; we have also taken from the one near Mr. F. N. Fisk's house, some five feet of clay. There are others which should be cleaned out. The reservoir near the South Church was drained in about 15 or 20 minutes, at Mr. Chandler's fire. We are of opinion that a drain running from Messrs. Clough and Corning's Block, and near that reservoir, must have injured it very much.

The places where reservoirs are most needed at this time, in the opinion of the Board of Engineers, are as follows : A reservoir is needed very much indeed on the hill, near Mr. A. B. Holt. There is located in that vicinity one hundred thousand dollars worth of taxable property, without any protection in the shape of a reservoir, in case of fire. The Board of Engineers have received estimates showing that a reservoir of sufficient capacity to supply two engines for two hours, could be built and supplied with water for $475 or $500; and they are of opinion that one should be built as soon as possible. They would also recommend that one be built at the corner of Spring and Centre streets. A reservoir is very much needed in Fisherville, on the hill west of the village. A plank reservoir could, in the opinion of the Board, be built for 100 dollars, and perhaps less, and the citizens will supply it with water without any expense to the city. The Board recommend the building of one in that place.

With regard to the sum paid annually to the firemen, the Board would recommend that it be paid in instalments of 17 cents per month, for the time they belong to the company, to avoid difficulties which exist at the present time with regard to their pay.

I would tender my sincere thanks to the Board of Engineers for their prompt and efficient aid on all occasions. I would do the same also to all the firemen composing the different companies; they have done their duty on all occasions with promptness and efficiency.

The apparatus has been kept by the stewards of the different companies to the entire satisfaction of the Board of Engineers.

All which is respectfully submitted.

OSCAR G. INGALLS, CHIEF ENGINEER.

The following are the names of the members of the Fire Department at the present time :

BOARD OF ENGINEERS.

Oscar G. Ingalls, Chief Engineer; Leonard Drown, James Frye, Moses Humphrey, B. H. Lincoln, A. B. Holt, Lowell Eastman, James L. Mason, Luther P. Fuller, Assistant Engineers.

ENGINE COMPANY, No. 2.—Concord—*Members :*—H. H. Holt, R. M. Ordway, W. T. Locke, George Dame, Joseph Brown, F. La Bontee, James Morrill, C. H. Herbert, C. C. Hartford, S. M. Griffin, John A. West, Wm. Roby, Calvin Smart, H. P. Sweetser, L. A. Walker, G. W. Emerton, D. Kennedy, George Brackett, John Richardson, M. H. Bradley, John M. Hill, Moses C. Hadley, John M. Bowker, V. R. Moore, Henry Dunlap, Harrison Roby, J. D. Emerson, Hiram Richardson, Guy S. Rix, George T. Carter, James W. Follansby, Richard K. Gatley, Wm. Kenney, Francis Dow, Charles Ash, Wm. L. Robinson, Otis Hardy, J. Ryder, Benjamin F. Roby, James W. Teel, Wm. Smith, Charles Pettengill, George Simons, E. B. Robinson, Andrew Saltmarsh, George B.

Roby, Daniel Nichols, J. Labonta, Rufus Bacon, M. D. Drew, J. B. Favour, James G. Leighton, John B. Leighton, Henry A. Chellis. LUTHER ROBY, JR., *Foreman.* C. H. BURR, *Clerk.*

ENGINE COMPANY, No. 3.—Joseph Meyers, James M. Otis, Chas. H. Abbott, James Thompson, Daniel H. Stokes, Edward Sanborn, Charles Butters, Charles E. Thompson, Andrew J. Tilton, Charles Bradley, Oliver Turner, Leander C. Lull, Dudley Winslow, Jesse Lull, Joseph Whitney, Jeremiah Batchelder, Charles McMichael, Alvin Kimball, William Page, Sylvanus Adams, Sydney Upham, Joseph Labonta, Joseph Blake, Baxter Blake, Charles T. Summers, Samuel McCawley, Joshua Lane, George W. Bean, Asa Rust, Charles Crow, Joseph Lane, James Morrison, Robert Blake, James Stevens, John Geenty, Joshua Kendall, Joel Dow, J. K. Stokes, Joseph J. Pillsbury, N. S. Pillsbury, W. E. Morton, Job M. Cook, Thomas Upham, Daniel S. Webster, E. C. Downs, A. J. Langley, William Williamson, John J. Mills, Josiah Cooper, Charles S. Colby, Sullivan Mills, George W. Boyden, Charles Willson, George F. Buzzel, Joseph Lamprey, M. H. Johnson, Thomas Harnden, Jacob H. Cook, N. W. Gove, John R. Scales.

CALEB PARKER, *Foreman.* JAMES M. OTIS, *Clerk.*

ENGINE COMPANY, No. 4.—Joseph Kezer, James G. Alexander, James Goodspeed, J. Frank Hoit, James Davis, Nelson Tenney, J. C. Dunklee, C. C. Webster, W. G. Shaw, Jeremiah Brown, Ira F. Morse, S. D. Greeley, John D. Teel, Samuel Edmunds, J. W. Prescott, Charles E. Mead, Wm. S. Davis, David B. Rowe, John S. Webster, Alonzo H. Morrison, C. F. Lane, Calvin Gerrish, S. L. Sanders, Henry H. Arlin, David Brown, Jr., B. F. Wolcott, Chas. H. Dunklee, Prescott F. Stevens, Arthur L. Davis, Geo. W. Stone, T. O. Gardner, Benj. Leighton, John Leighton, John F. Scott, Joseph Elkins, A. S. Granger, Frank H. Lock, S. W. French, J. M. Jones, Levi Call, Daniel S. Ripley, Warren C. Webster, Patrick Morrison, Rufus Meyers, Jacob B. Wiggin, Patrick Clary, Moody P. Davis.

JONATHAN SARGENT, *Foreman.* NATHANIEL J. MEAD, *Clerk.*

ENGINE COMPANY, No. 6.—Chandler Eastman, John Quinn, B. F. Holden, Moses F. Clough, B. F. Dow, Joseph Eastman, Geo. W. Brown, Hiram Farnum, Wm. H. Brown, Charles H. Clough, E. C. Ferrin, Daniel Marden, Stephen W. Kellom, Lyman Sawyer, Thomas S. Gow, Michael Huben, Rufus Abbott, J. N. Speed, O. A. Williams, Gust Williams, Harrison Partridge, Jackson Crosby, Patrick Owens, George Partridge, A. H. Baker, M. D. Dodge, An-

42

drew Crockett, Jr., Wyman Holden, A. L. Marden, George W.
Cheever, John Harrington, George W. Shepard, John Jenkins, Benj.
Brock, Michael Jenkins, George Jones, B. F. Varney, John Thorn-
ton, George Ladd, Chester Darling, Asaph Abbott, Joseph Palmer,
Joseph Taylor, Michael Kelley, Wm. T. Speed, John Giles, Amos
S. Abbot.

MOSES HUMPHREY, *Foreman*.   J. CROSBY, *Clerk*.

ENGINE COMPANY, No. 7.—William Page, James M. Carleton,
Adoniram B. Seavey, Winthrop St. Clair, Smith Bean, Lewis Bean,
James Frye, Gardner Tenney, George W. Moody, James Sanborn,
James Smith, Washington Hill, John T. Batchelder, Cyrus Farrar,
George W. Moulton, William Pecker, Benjamin P. Kimball, Samuel
Moody, George Turner, Jacob Clough, Timothy W. Emery, Warren
A. Bean, John Hutchins, John C. Hutchins, Joseph Clough, Peter
C. Virgin, Charles H. Sanborn, Alfred E. Emery, Joseph Dow,
Horace Ames, Joseph Duplissis, Benjamin Morrill, George B. Peck-
er, John Hill.

HEMAN SANBORN, *Foreman*.   CYRUS R. ROBINSON, *Clerk*.

ENGINE COMPANY, No. 8.—Fisherville—Abial Rolfe, John A. Co-
burn, David A. Brown, Leonard Drown, Isaac G. Howe, Samuel
R. Flanders, Charles W. Hardy, William H. Allen, Nathaniel
Rolfe, Hazen Knowlton, Samuel C. Pickard, Charles L. Bach-
elder, Jacob B. Rand, Timothy C. Rolfe, Charles Abbot,
Nathan Emerson, Jeremiah S. Durgin, Benj. Morrill, Albert
L. Smith, Daniel W. Martin, Edward McArdle, Geo. H. Hinton,
Daniel Gibson, Frederick Flanders, Joshua S. Bean, Charles D.
Rowell, Frank Morse, Timothy H. Potter, Martin Sargent, John G.
Warren, James K. Bricket, William E. Woodward, Charles Smith,
E. F. Bachelder, Geo. S. Danforth, John Whitaker, Moses H. Bean,
Charles J. Ellsworth, Mason W. Tucker, William W. Flanders,
Robert Crowther, E. S. Harris, Alonzo Morgan, John A. Kilburn,
Samuel R. Mann, George B. Elliot, Sylvester G. Long.

ALBERT H. DROWN, *Foreman*.   S. MERRIAM, *Clerk*.

HOOK & LADDER COMPANY, No. 1.—John C. Hall, Harry
Houston, Frederick S. Crawford, Edson C. Eastman, Jos. B. Smart,
John L. Gordon, Thos. B. Jones, Curtis White, S. N. Farnsworth,
Isaac A. Hill, Josiah B. Sanborn, Gust Walker, J. L. Cilley, John
C. Pillsbury, Robert Crummett, Jeremiah Smith, J. P. Wheeler, J.
G. Elliott, Jos. Leahy, C. C. Shaw, John Miller, Daniel Clough,
Geo. A. Dow, D. D. Brainard, N. S. Shaw, J. F. Cotton, Geo. Page,
Wm. H. Wyman, Abr. S. Sanborn, Henry E. Mirick, Michael

Arnold, Jos. H. Sanders, John E. Shaw, A. W. Rix, J. M: Prentiss,
T. K. Blaisdell, Michael Haines, Cyrus Clough, M. H. Sawin,
Stephen Sweatt, Joseph Sweatt, Geo. S. Dennett, R. W. Willey, E.
A. Miller, Moses Sweatt, Jos. N. Carter, Martin Keenan, E. B.
Hutchinson, E. W. Gove.

JOHN C. HALL, *Foreman.*   FRED. S. CRAWFORD, *Clerk.*

REPORTS OF THE LIQUOR AGENT.

To the Mayor and Aldermen of the City of Concord:

The undersigned respectfully submits the following report of
his agency in purchase and sale of liquors in the city of Concord,
from May 1st, 1858, to February 1st, 1859. (Nine months.)

Amount of liquors on hand, May 1st, 1858,	$510·00
" " " since purchased,	3,270·81
" " freight, analyzing, rent, etc.,	221·53
" " agent's salary, 9 months,	225·00
" " net profits,	458·88
	$4686·22

CONTRA:

Amount of liquors on hand, Feb. 1st, 1859,	$1015·81
Amount of sales to date,	3580·41
Loss in value of liquors rec'd from former agent,	90·00
	$4686·22

Whole amount of sales to date,	$3580·41
Amount sold to agents,	394·38
" sold at retail	3186·03

Whole number of sales, 11070.

CASH ACCOUNT.

Whole amount of receipts to date,	$3580·41

Accounted for as follows:

Paid R. E. Pecker, on old account,	$371·94
Seth E. Pecker,	1474·57
D. W. Lawrence,	516·94
C. H. Curtice,	26·24
A. W. Chellis,	21·00
E. A. Boardman,	707·75
H. B. Foster, for bottles,	12·28

Freight, analyzing, rent, etc.,   221·53
Salary of agent,   225·00
                                  $3577·25

Cash on hand, $3·16
Present indebtedness of the agency, $468·16.

JOEL C. DANFORTII, AGENT.

STATE OF NEW HAMPSHIRE.

MERRIMACK, ss. *February 10th*, 1859. Then personally appeared Joel C. Danforth, and made oath that the above report by him subscribed was true. BEFORE ME:

JOHN Y. MUGRIDGE, *Justice of the Peace.*

REPORT OF LIQUOR AGENT AT FISHERVILLE.

To the Mayor and Aldermen of the City of Concord:

The undersigned respectfully submits the following report of his agency in the purchase and sale of wines and spirituous liquors at Fisherville, in the city of Concord, from May 3d, 1858, to January 29th, 1859 :

Amount of wines and liquors on hand, May 3d, 1858,	$30·86
Amount of wines and liquors since purchased,	321·36
" " freight bills,	6·90
" " agent's service,	112·50
	$471·62

CONTRA:

Amount of liquors and wines on hand, Jan. 29th, 1859,	$24·07
" " sales of liquors and wines to date,	404·10
" " casks,	8·80
" " casks, jugs, and measures on hand,	20·63
	$457·60

Whole number of sales, 1845.

Respectfully submitted,

ANDREW A. DOW, AGENT.

MERRIMACK, ss. *January 29th*, 1859. Subscribed and sworn to before me,   ALBERT H. DROWN, JUSTICE OF THE PEACE.

REPORT OF THE POLICE JUSTICE.

To the Mayor and Aldermen of the City of Concord:

In compliance with the city charter, the undersigned respectfully submits the following report:

During the last financial year the whole number of entries upon the civil docket of the Police Court is   40

The whole number of entries upon the criminal docket is   114

In the criminal cases the offences charged are as follows, to wit:

Assault and battery,	22
Selling intoxicating liquor,	18
Keeping for sale intoxicating liquor,	6
Keeping restaurant without license,	9
Larceny,	9
Disorderly conduct,	6
Feloniously breaking & entering houses & other buildings,	7
Intoxication,	6
Violating the ordinance relative to stallions,	3
Not closing restaurant at ten o'clock in the evening,	3
Adultery,	2
Fornication,	2
Playing with cards,	2
Threatening to do harm to other persons,	2
Obtaining goods by false pretences,	2
Making false statement to the city agent for selling liquor,	1
Aiding in the escape of a prisoner from jail,	1
Common drunkard,	2
Common pilferer,	1
Selling beer in a restaurant on Sunday,	1
Resisting a police officer,	1
Maliciously injuring the real estate of another person,	1
Keeping a gaming place,	1
Making a noise, brawl and tumult,	3
Keeping a disorderly house,	1
Robbing a garden,	1
Attempting to rescue a prisoner,	1
Total,	—114

Of the foregoing were sentenced to pay fines,   52
Ordered to recognize to appear at S. J. Court,   39
Dismissed or nol. pros.   9
Sentenced to House of Correction,   7
Discharged,   3
Ordered to find sureties to keep the peace,   2
Sentenced to House of Reformation,   1
Sentenced to jail,   1
     Total,   —114

Notwithstanding the provisions of the second section of the ·¹·· entitled, " An act in amendment of the charter of the city of Concord," passed last June, the Special Justice has not filed with the justice of the Police Court any writ, warrant or original process in any cause, which has been tried or entered before him. And the irregularity and inconvenience still continue of having parts of the original records or files of the court permanently kept in two places and by different persons.

The undersigned charges himself as Police Justice with the amount of fines received during said year, $216·00
    Amount of fees and costs,   193·05

                                   $409·00

And discharges himself as follows, to wit :
    Paid for printing blanks, $8·12
    Paid City Treasurer,   400·93

                                     $409·05

                  DAVID PILLSBURY, POLICE JUSTICE.
Concord, Jan. 31, 1850.

REPORT OF SPECIAL POLICE JUSTICE.

To the Mayor and Aldermen of the City of Concord:

The following is a true and correct exhibition of all moneys received by me, in the capacity of Special Justice, agreeably to the statute of this State, chapter 2120, passed June 24th, 1858.

Oct. 13, 1857. 1. State vs. Mark Town, (bound over.) Larceny.
  Costs.   Fees received, $1·91
Jan. 27, 1858. 2. Ellen Welch vs. Philip Welcome. (Bastardy.)
  (bound over.)   Fees received, 1·17
Feb. 27, 1858. 3. Cyrus Peaslee vs. Charles C. Clark, and Trs. Assumpsit.
                                                    Costs, 1·76
July 19, 1858, 4. State vs. James Spain. Fine, $2·00, cost, $1·59, $3·59
July 19, 1858, 5. State vs. John Pickett. Fine, $2·00, cost, $1·59, 3·59
July 28, 1858, 6. State vs. Daniel Sullivan. Cost,   1·35
                                                             ———
                                                           $13·37

S. C. BADGER, *Special Justice Police Court.*

CONCORD, January 29th, 1859.

The CITY OF CONCORD to STEPHEN C. BADGER, DR.

Oct. 13, 1857, to 1 day's service as Special Justice, Police Court,	$2·00
Feb. 27, 1858, to 1 " " " " " "	2·00
March, " " 1 " " " " " "	2·00
July 19, 1858, 1 day's " " " " "	2·00
July 28, 1858, 1 day's " " " " "	2·00
July 30, 1858, 1 day's " " " " "	2·00
August 14, 1858, 1 day's " " " " "	2·00

                                                           $16·00
Cr. by cash received for costs and fines,   13·37
                                                           ———
            Balance, $2·63
RECEIVED PAYMENT, by order on the City Treasurer, as above.

S. C. BADGER.

REPORT OF THE TRUSTEES OF THE PUBLIC LIBRARY.

[For the year ending Jan. 27, 1859.]

A good measure of prosperity has attended the City Library, during the past year. Its records show a good number of subscribers, and the books upon its shelves have been sought with an avidity that attests the indispensableness of the institution to supply the intellectual wants of our community. The usefulness of the library has been somewhat hindered by the lack of means to supply it with many books, the possession of which is desirable. However, the Trustees have attempted to make the most of the means at their disposal, and have, from time to time, made such additions to the Library, as were most imperatively demanded.

During the past year, 410 volumes have been added by purchase, and 76 by donation. The total number of volumes now in the Library is 2778. Of these 2162 volumes are for general reading and circulation, and 616 are more particularly adapted for reference, having been donated to the Library at sundry times. By the Treasurer's report it appears that $228·16 has been expended for books ; to this amount should be added the sum of about $70 upon orders drawn but not paid at the time the report was made, making a total of $298·16.

The other principal expenses for the year have been the Catalogue, (the sales of which will in time, make full reimbursement), the rebinding of books, and the compensation of the Librarian. For the payment of the Librarian and the rebinding of books, (which last item has amounted, the last year to $90·28,) it may be safe to rely upon subscriptions and fines. But to obtain the proper yearly supplies of books, the institution must look to other sources. During the past year the Library has received an appropriation of $50 from the city Treasury. If the Library is to be properly sustained, and made to answer at all the purposes for which it was established, an appropriation of at least $300 a year must be made for some years, by the city government, for its benefit. The expected gifts of money from certain persons who have intimated their purpose of making bestowments upon the Library, have not yet been received, and it is a matter of uncertainty when they will be. Until they be received, the Library must look for maintenance in respect of the supply of books to the city government that brought it into existence. In every other city, the Public Library is the object of liberal annual appropriations, shall it be an exception in this ?

The following are some of the principal donations of books during the past year:

One Mass., Agricultural Report 1857; 1 Ohio Agricultural Report, 1857; 1 Maine Agricultural Report, 1857; 1 Maine Agricultural Reports 1856; 6 vols., New Hampshire Agricultural Report, to 1857. by J. C. A. Wingate, Esq. ; 2 copies " Another Budget"; 1 Christmas Gift; 1 Sarah Barry's Home; 1, My Mother's Jewels, from Mrs. J. A. Eames ; 1 Salad for the Social; 1 Salad for the Solitary, by Charles Minot Esq. ; 1 N. P. Rogers' Writing, by R. C. Osgood; 1 Writings of W. Loyd Garrison ; 1 Emerson's Representative Men ; 7 vols. Theodore Parker's Works, from Nathaniel White, Esq. ; 1 vol. Smithsonian Report, 1858, from the Secretary.

As to the financial condition of the Library we refer to the account of the Treasurer, E. S. Towle, Esq., herewith appended.

TREASURER'S REPORT.

DR. *Concord Public Library* in acc't with *E. S. Towle*, TR. CR.

1858. CASH PAID:—		1858.	
Jan. 26, S. Clark & Brown,	$89·28	Jan. 23, by balance,	$401·86
"　" E. C. Eastman,	20·29	March 23, by Cash,	25·00
April 2, F. S. Crawford,	50·73	May 8,　"　"	36·00
May 7, Jones & Cogswell,	4·75	" 31,　"　"	20·00
"　" E. C. Eastman,	77·53	Oct. 15,　"　"	50·00
"　"　"　"	16·67	Jan. 9, 1859, by cash,	39·00
June 28, Fogg & Hadley,	80·00	" 27,　"　"　"	12·00
July 19, F. S. Crawford,	53·05		
Oct. 26, Crosby & Nichols,	84·39		
Jan. 26, 1859, F. S. Crawford,	79·20		
" 27, " A. Hadley,	2·20		
Balance carried forward,	25·77		$583·86
	$583·86	Jan. 27, 1859, by balance,	$25·77

(Errors excepted.) January 27, 1859.

E. S. TO WLE, TREASURER CONCORD PUBLIC LIBRARY.

4

REPORT OF COMMITTEE ON CITY HALL.

The Committee appointed March 15, 1851, to purchase land, and in conjunction with the county of Merrimack, to cause to be erected thereon, and on land of said county, a suitable Court House, and City Hall, respectfully

REPORT:

That they purchased for the aforesaid purpose, of John W. Noyes, the Dearborn lot, so called, for the sum of ($6330) sixty-three hundred and thirty dollars ; of the late Nathan Stickney, another adjoining tract of land, for the sum of one dollar ; and at a later date of Seth Eastman, Agent, the McDaniel estate for the sum of ($1163) eleven hundred and sixty-three dollars.

That they subsequently concluded an agreement with said county for the erection of a Court House and City Hall, upon this and land of said county ; said county to share equally with the city of Concord the expense of erecting said building, which agreement is now on record in the office of the Register of Deeds of said county.

That not long afterwards in conjunction with said county, they made contracts with different parties for the construction of said building as follows, to wit, with Luther Roby & Son for the stone work, with Henry M. Robinson for the brick work, with A. Webster & Son, for the carpenters' work, with William K. Holt for timber, with Amos Bean, Joseph R. Bowers, Philip Sargent, and A. & D. L. Holt, for bricks, and with Henry M. Morse, for the completion of said building. For the terms and specifications of said contracts you are respectfully referred to the several instruments now on file in the office of the clerk of the court for said county.

The expenditures made by this committee for excavations, drains, grading of lot, erecting, finishing and furnishing of said building, have been ($31·713·04) thirty-one thousand seven hundred and thirteen dollars and four cents, as follows, to wit :

Paid as follows :		Paid as follows :	
Fife & Holt, excavation,	$463·10	J. E. Brown, lumber,	60·27
A. B. Holt, grading, drawing		Moore & Cilley, hardware,	10·06
stone, &c.,	82·85	J. C. Whittemore, masonry,	77·60
L. Roby & Sons, stone work,	4,244·53	C. H. Norton, labor,	7·50
Norton & Fife, drain,	1,280·15	D. H. Fletcher, carpenters work,	794·85
Cornelius Driscol, labor,	7·50	S. G. Austin, lightning rods,	52·06
Michael Larkin, "	10·50	G. W. Fitts, blacksmiths work,	27·21
Thomas Clark, "	3·00	Nath'l Ray, furniture for hall,	187·32
A. A. Currier, "	11·50	C. W. Batchelder, labor,	1·86
Joseph R. Bowers, bricks,	525·50	J. F. Morse, gas pipes,	207·85
N. Railroad, transportation,	6·00	Eli Dodge, services,	52·50
Emerson & Cutting, lumber,	6·01	P. Carey, upholstery,	14·75
Henry M. Robinson, masonry,	3·508·01	Sanborn & Jackson, carpeting,	113·64
J. L. Foster, Architect & Supt.	462·50	Whitney & Bros., gas fixtures,	393·95
Barton & Hadley, printing,	1·71	Wm. T. Putnam, gas fitting,	45·74
Smart and Sewall, teaming,	95·31	G. Sanders & Co., stoves, funnels,	171·68
Amos Bean, books,	402·60	D. A. Hill, furniture,	177·75
W. P. & T. H. Ford, iron work,	559·25	D. Clifford, labor,	1·25
Philip Sargent, bricks,	759·50	D. M. Carpenter, services,	10·00
Nathan Wiser, labor,	3·50	Charles C. Burr, labor,	3·25
Seth Eastman, agent, land,	1,163·00	G. D. Abbott, painting settees,	92·88
J. B. Hook, brick,	418·20	J. Abbott, services and bills paid,	63·62
Joseph Low, services,	50·00	Geo. Hutchins, cement,	25·35
William K. Holt, lumber,	1,004·68	A. J. Hook, labor,	7·50
A. & D. L. Holt, brick,	1,932·75	J. I. Lund, labor and fixtures of	
J. L. Foster, agent, terra cotta,	371·12	water closet,	56·53
H. M. Moore, joiner's work,	9,873·77	D. A. Warde, hardware,	42·08
A. Webster & Son, carpenter's		David Hoag, slating,	48·16
work,	633·42	C. Treas., balance on settlement,	41·86
Tolman, Hathaway & Stone,		G. D. & W. B. Abbott, painting,	16·54
terra cotta,	452·43	S. M. Chesley, blacksmith's work,	1·61
Rufus Clement, labor, &c.,	66·18	Geo. W. Emerton, stone work,	156·83
A. B. Currier, ventilators,	37·87	Joseph P. Stickney, bricks,	16·35
Jones & Cogswell, printing,	12·50	Rixford & Bunker, windows,	29·50
John D. Fife, engineering,	29·00	James Straw, repairing roof,	55·22
C. Railroad, transportation,	84	Geo. A. Pillsbury,	4·87
Smith & Dumas, labor,	15·00	J. Abbott, for grading and split-	
Wm. H. Bartlett, legal service,	5·00	ting stone,	1,238·62
D. S. Webster, teaming,	38·25		
J. Noyes, masonry,	30·36		$31,713·04

There is an unsettled claim of H. M. Moore, not included in the above. The nominal amount is $2·178, but it is believed that the sum which has been offered him in settlement ($700) covers all which is justly due, one half of this claim is to be paid by the county.

All of which is respectfully submitted,

RICHARD BRADLEY, ⎫
JOSEPH B. WALKER, |
JOHN ABBOTT, |
J. MINOT, ⎬ COMMITTEE.
DAN'L H. FLETCHER, |
JOSEPH LOW. ⎭

Concord, Feb. 12, 1859.